ABOUT THE AUTHOR

When Geoffrey McSkimming was a boy he
found an old motion-picture projector and a tin
containing a dusty film in his grandmother's attic.
He screened the film and was transfixed by
the flickering image of a man in a jaunty pith helmet,
baggy Sahara shorts and special desert sun-spectacles.
The man had an imposing macaw and a clever looking
camel, and Geoffrey McSkimming was mesmerised
by their activities in black-and-white Egypt, Peru,
Greece, Mexico, Sumatra, Turkey, Italy and
other exotic locations.

Years later he discovered the identities of the trio,
and has spent much of his time since then retracing
their footsteps, interviewing surviving members of the
Old Relics Society, and gradually reconstructing these
lost true tales which have become the enormously
successful Cairo Jim chronicles.

Geoffrey McSkimming regards *Cairo Jim
and the Secret Sepulchre of the Sphinx* to be the most
mysterious story so far, and he lost a considerable
amount of hair while trying to work out what it was
that so puzzled Cairo Jim.

For Belinda,

who knows a lot of what is hidden

First published in Great Britain 2007 by Walker Books Ltd
87 Vauxhall Walk, London SE11 5HJ

2 4 6 8 10 9 7 5 3 1

Text © 1999 Geoffrey McSkimming
Cover illustration © 2007 Walker Books Ltd

This book has been typeset in Plantin

Printed in Great Britain by
Cox & Wyman Ltd, Reading, Berkshire

British Library Cataloguing in Publication Data:
a catalogue record for this book is available from the British Library.

ISBN 978-1-4063-0544-9

www.walkerbooks.co.uk

CAIRO JIM

AND THE SECRET SEPULCHRE
OF THE SPHINX

A Tale of Incalculable Inversion

GEOFFREY McSKIMMING

WALKER
BOOKS

▲▲▲▲▲ CONTENTS ▲▲▲▲▲

A WORD TO MY READERS

Archaeology, as anyone who is involved in it will tell you if you hang around for long enough, is a profession full of riddles and abounding with mysteries, as that well-known archaeologist and little-known poet, Cairo Jim, often found.

It is also an occupation full of uncertainty.

During my time researching the Cairo Jim Chronicles, never have I come across such a puzzling story as *Cairo Jim and the Secret Sepulchre of the Sphinx*. It is, perhaps, the most archaeological of all the chronicles so far. In attempting to recount what Jim, Doris the macaw, Brenda the Wonder Camel and Jocelyn Osgood went through – surrounded as they were by a blanket of mystery – I had moments of great frustration. I like to think it was the same sort of frustration felt by Jim and his friends, although mine was on a much smaller scale, I am sure.

Thanks to the prodigious archives kept at the Old Relics Society in Cairo, I was finally able to stumble across the answer to this mighty riddle. I hope that the story, as told here, does justice to the exploits of Jim of Cairo, and all his friends, and I hope you enjoy this "mystery of history".

G. McS.

Part One:

A THOUSAND PACES...

DIGGING FOR
WE KNOW NOT WHAT

"EVER SINCE THE DEATH of Neptune Bone, things have certainly been calm and sweet and restful, don't you think? Raark!"

By the south-flung shadow of the Pyramid of Chephren at Giza, on the outskirts of Cairo, the beautiful yellow-and-blue-feathered macaw known as Doris was perching happily on her mahogany stand, casting a contented, beady eye over the sands before her.

"Quaaaooo," came a snorting reply. Brenda the Wonder Camel looked up from her Melodious Tex western adventure novel and rolled her head in agreement. Her long eyelashes fluttered in the rising heat of the morning.

Doris opened her huge wings and closed them again. "Yes siree," she chirped. "Since Bone dropped off the twig, we haven't had much to worry about at all. No evilness, no rudeness, no yucky cigar smoke or wretchedly decorated fezzes to have to look at. No overblown threats of global domination or the resurrection of ancient, long-forgotten gods. Not to mention any exposure to that vile, stinking fleabag raven of his."

"And Jim's been able to get on with some real archaeological delvings," Brenda thought in her Wonder Camel telepathic way.

"And Jim's been able to get on with some real archaeological delvings," said Doris, picking up on her friend's thought. "Look at him down there, Brenda."

Brenda peered through the heat haze.

"He's as happy as a ... as happy as a ... reeerk ... he's as happy as a very happy man standing waist-deep in a hole of his own making in the middle of the Giza plateau. A man and his work. There are some things, don't you think, Bren, that are just meant to be?"

"Quaaaooo," snorted the Wonder Camel.

Cairo Jim, that well-known archaeologist and little-known poet, was indeed waist-deep in a hole of his own making. Every now and then he bobbed down until only the crown of his pith helmet was visible above the sand. Then he'd stand upright, the top of his shovel appearing quickly, and a spray of sand would fly up into the air. And then he'd bob down again.

"Dig, dig, dig," Doris crooned, as the mid-morning sunlight cast a soft but brilliant glow onto her plumage.

Brenda swished her tail at a wasp that was buzzing a little too close for comfort.

She, Doris and Cairo Jim had been camping here, far north of their home campsite in the Valley of the Kings, for almost a fortnight. She was beginning to miss things from home: her favourite, secret patch of sand where she could relax, unbothered, beneath a shady date palm and lose herself in her western adventure novels; the open-air courtyard of Mrs Amun-Ra's Tea Rooms in the nearby village of Gurna, where Jim took her and Doris for cakes and worms (Brenda had a passion for worms); and the quiet, star-twinkling nights when the wind blew through the tombs of ancient Kings and Queens, Nobles and Hairdressers, Schoolteachers and Ice-Cream Vendors (some discovered and others waiting to be discovered) – a wind sounding like cavernous whispers from a great, cobwebbed past.

Since Captain Neptune F. Bone had been carted away for the last time by the Sphinx of the Naxians, there had been time to enjoy these things.

But then the letter had arrived, and Jim had brought Brenda and Doris north to this place.

The Wonder Camel was thinking about all of this, when a new thought struck her with such suddenness that her mane bristled and stood on end. "Just what *exactly* is Jim digging for?" she silently wondered. "*Why are we here?*"

"*Reerraarrk!*" Doris screeched loudly, and hop-fluttered about on her perch.

In the distant haze, Jim popped his head up, looked across at her and Brenda, and waved his hand. Then he returned to his digging.

"Do you know, Bren," Doris spluttered, "I've just realised something. Plait my plumes, I don't know why it'd never occurred to me before!"

"Quaaaooo?" Brenda snorted.

"Tell me this: just what *exactly* is Jim digging for? *Why are we here?*"

Brenda shrugged, scraping a hoof in the sand.

"He hasn't told us, has he?" The macaw blinked her small, dark eyes rapidly. "No, he hasn't. He just said one afternoon that we had to come north for a while to start a new dig. After that urgent letter came from Gerald Perry Esquire. Remember, Bren?"

Brenda opened her jaws to snort a reply, but Doris kept on going.

"Hmmph. It's incredible, don't you think, how Gerald Perry Esquire can make Jim stop everything and go all over the place at the drop of a pith helmet?"

"Perry is a very good patron to us," Brenda thought, rolling her head in a circle. "He always looks after us and makes sure we have enough funding to do everything."

"But I s'pose," clucked Doris, "that he *is* a good patron to us. He always looks after us, and that sort of thing."

"Quaaaooo."

"Be that as it may." Doris arched her crestfeathers forward. "Jim still hasn't told us what we're all doing up here. Reeerk! It'd be nice to know what's going on, don't you reckon?"

Brenda fluttered her eyelashes in a 'yes' fashion.

"Fancy, a grown bird and a grown Wonder Camel coming all this way without knowing why. Without knowing what the purpose is. It seems we are in the dark, Brenda. It seems that we are being kept apart 'from all direction, purpose, course, intent', to quote Mr Shakespeare's *King John*."

Brenda nodded, and flicked her tail.

"Well," said Doris, her feathers taking on a determined, investigative quality, "I'm going to find out why. I'll just go on over and ask Jim himself. Myself. *Our*self. Oh, for squawking out loud! See you soon."

She lifted her wings, rose into the air, and soared off across the small dunes.

The Wonder Camel watched her approach Jim's dig.

Doris hovered for a moment, still and quietly, directly above the hole, then folded her wings in and dropped quickly to the ground. Seconds before her talons were to scrape into the sand, she made a small arc, and came to land gracefully and silently behind the bent figure of Cairo Jim.

Brenda gave a small snort of admiration at her little friend's flying prowess, and returned to her novel.

"*SQQQUUUUUUEEEEEAAAAAR-RRRRRRRRAAAAARRRRRRKKKK*!" Doris let off a screech so loud that several clouds, far up in the sky, changed their courses.

"*AAAAAAAaaaaaaaaaarrrrrrrrrrrkkkkkk!*" cried Jim, leaping into the air and almost out of the hole. He turned, the shovel in his hand trembling, and saw Doris staring at him. "My dear!" he gasped. "I wish you wouldn't sneak up on me like that."

"My apologies." She crossed her wings across her

breast-plumage. "Jim, there's something that Brenda and I would like to know."

The archaeologist-poet put down the shovel and took his handkerchief from his pocket. "Oh, yes? What's that?" He reached up into his knapsack at the rim of the hole and took out his water bottle.

"Well, it's just occurred to us that we don't know why we're here. What are we digging for?"

Jim poured some of the water onto his handkerchief and rubbed the cool fabric across his forehead, cheeks and chin. "Good question," he replied, slipping the handkerchief under his pith helmet and arranging it flat on his hair.

"Good question?" Doris blinked curiously.

"It is," Jim nodded. He took off his special desert sun-spectacles and started cleaning them on the hem of his shirt. "We're digging for we know not what."

"*Whatnots?* What do we want with whatnots? Rerk! There're plenty of whatnots in the Cairo Museum and in the Old Relics Society and all around the—"

"No, Doris, not whatnots. We're digging for we know *not what*."

"You mean that *you* don't know why we're here either?"

"I'm afraid that's right."

Doris started to pace up and down in the sand. "So we've come all this way, we've left the Valley of the Kings and all our digging down there – where at least there's the chance of finding a tomb or something – to be *here*, with the curtain of uncertainty billowing all around us?"

"That's a nice phrase, my dear." Jim put his sun-spectacles back on and smiled at her. "The curtain of uncertainty billowing all around us. Yes. May I use that in a poem tonight?"

"Jim! This is nothing to do with poetry! Do you mean to say you have no idea what we're looking for here on the Giza plateau?"

Jim sighed. "No idea at all, Doris."

"But that letter Perry sent you! Surely he told you in that?"

"No, he didn't. Look, have a read for yourself." He undid the button on one of his shirt pockets and withdrew the folded sheet of lemon-coloured parchment paper that Perry had sent. This he unfolded and laid on the ground in front of the macaw. "Go on, read it out loud."

Doris squinted at the spidery handwriting on the paper. "Hmm. He's sent it from Cairo. From the Old Relics Society. Dated five weeks ago."

"Read it."

She cleared her throat and carefully enunciated:

Dear Jim, Doris, Brenda,
A startling revelation! Have found something of <u>immense</u> <u>possibility</u>, a clue of <u>ancient monumental proportions</u>, here in the Old Relics Society library. Can't say too much now, for fear of this letter

CAIRO JIM AND THE SECRET SEPULCHRE OF THE SPHINX

getting stolen or lost. But you all must go at once to the Pyramid of Chephren & start digging exactly one thousand paces due south of the Pyramid.

I'm leaving some money & a new tent & camping supplies for you at the Society, so don't bring all your stuff up from the Valley of the Kings. Unfortunately I won't be round for a month or so – the day after tomorrow I have to go on another of those silly cruises to Suva again, made the bookings a while ago & can't get out of it – but come and see me at the Society after the eighteenth, when I'm back.

This is so exciting (the clue I've found, not the cruise – I hate shuffleboard & having to play those infernal games like Pin the Tail on the Donkey – last time I got so dizzy when they spun me round I stuck the stupid thing into the ship's purser, who didn't seem to mind for some reason, in fact for the rest of the voyage he kept going HEE-HAW, HEE-HAW! very loudly whenever he saw me on deck, which was far too often for my liking).

Anyway, it's so very exciting that I have to go & have a calming little rest in the Sarcophagus Chambers downstairs.

See you after the eighteenth, & if you haven't found anything by then, I'll tell you more.

Your good friend,

Gerald Perry (Esquire)

Doris looked up at Jim. "How strange," she cooed.

"Yes, but then again, maybe a lot of ships' pursers have a thing for donkeys. Perhaps the sea brings it out in them, all that salt air, or—"

"No, Jim, I mean this thing he's discovered in the library. This clue."

"Oh, yes." Jim wiped the perspiration from the back of his neck. "It must be something huge, to get Perry writing like that. What'd he say? *Immense possibility!*"

"A clue of *ancient monumental proportions*." Doris nodded.

"Perry wouldn't write like that unless he were genuinely thrilled at what it might be. He only ever sends us out to find something if it'll be truly worth the effort. That's why, when I read the letter, I had no doubts it must be important, and wasted no time in bringing us all up to Giza."

"Rark," rarked the bird.

Jim pulled himself up out of the hole, and sat, cross-legged, next to her. "But we haven't found anything, have we? Only sand and rocks and stones. It'd be a great help if we had some sort of inkling of what we're looking for. If it's a bit of ancient pottery, for example, or a rare coin, or something small and fragile, well, I'm going about it in the wrong way. I shouldn't be using that big shovel, for a start."

"Jim, what date is it today?"

He thought for a second. "The nineteenth. Tuesday the nineteenth. Doris, he's back!"

"Rerark."

"What time is it? I left my Cutterscrog Old Timers Archaeological Timepiece in the tent so it wouldn't get sand in it."

"Lend me your pith helmet," Doris said. "I'll tell you the time."

Cairo Jim looked puzzled, but took off his hat and handed it to her. She held it in one wing and raised it above her beak, so that it was between her and the eastern sky. "Hmm," she said, squinting through one of the six small ventilation holes in the top of the pith helmet. "It's eleven thirty-four exactly."

"Well swoggle me with a sundial," muttered Jim. He looked out at the sky, with the hot sun blazing away, and the haze shimmering off the sands and distant rooftops like trembling, ghostly vapours. "How can you tell?"

Doris passed the pith helmet back to him, the feathers around the edge of her beak wrinkling into what was, for macaws, a smile. "C'mon, buddy-boy, let's saddle up Brenda and head into Cairo, to the Old Relics Society."

"I never cease to be amazed," he said, standing, as the clever bird fluttered up onto his shoulder and they headed back to the tent.

△△△△△ 2 △△△△△
A LEG IN

AS BRENDA CANTERED through the traffic in Talaat Harb Street in Cairo, and as the cream-coloured granite pillars at the entrance to the Old Relics Society came into view, Jim could tell that something was out of the ordinary.

"Look, up there on top of the steps," he said to Doris, who was sitting in front of him, on the saddle's pommel. "Between the pillars. What's going on?"

"Rark! I haven't seen so many people at the Society since the day we discovered the tomb of Pharaoh Martenarten."

All around the pillars, and disappearing into the huge open doors of the Society's headquarters, hundreds of elderly women and gentlemen were swarming, all of them dressed in natty cream or off-white suits or dresses, some of them carrying walking sticks, some of them wearing straw fedora hats. As Jim, Doris and Brenda approached, it became obvious that some of the clothing had seen better days, but there was no untidiness amongst any of them; no matter how well-worn the suit or dress, every single man and woman up there on those steps had pressed their suit and cleaned their hat. There was not an unpolished shoe to be seen.

"It looks like a lot of Members have come especially for something. Come on, Brenda, my lovely, let's hurry!" Jim gave Brenda's sides a gentle nudge with his Sahara boots.

Brenda snorted and ascended the marble steps to the doors of the Old Relics Society.

In the massive entry vestibule, cool and dim and dotted here and there with gigantic ancient artefacts gathered from all around the world, things were squashy.

Doris cast her beady eye over all of the old gentlemen and the elderly women, all jostling shoulder-to-shoulder to be close to the huge reception bureau at the far end. "There's hardly enough room to swing a gnat," she observed.

"What do you think they're here for?" Jim asked, above the rising swell of excited voices.

"Search me." Doris shrugged her wings. "But whatever it is, it must be important."

Brenda, her nostrils flaring as she drew in whatever air she could after her journey, sensed something happening over at the reception bureau. "Listen," she snorted. "Someone's about to speak."

"Listen," Jim said, as Brenda's thought tingled through the saddle. "Someone's about to speak."

"Er-herm!" A strong but crackly voice came from the reception bureau, and almost immediately the crowd's noise fell to become a low sea of rippling murmurs.

"Ladies and gentlemen and everyone else," continued the voice, "welcome to the Old Relics

Society, on what is a day of mixed fortunes."

A large clump of Members moved away from the reception bureau, as the owner of the voice stepped up onto a small platform behind it.

"Look," whispered Jim. "It's Perry!"

Doris flexed herself up and down, and Brenda's ears bent forward.

"As one of the founding members of this august and dynamic Society, may I welcome you all here today." Gerald Perry Esquire, looking the nattiest of them all in his white linen suit and his freshly waxed moustache, beheld the crowd, his possum-like eyes regarding it solemnly but with a slight twinkle. At that moment, he saw Jim and Doris mounted high on Brenda, and he gave the three of them an affectionate nod.

"Thank you all for attending," he went on, addressing the crowd. "It is not often that we come together for an occasion such as this."

Many mutterings of 'It's about time, too,' 'I never thought I'd live to see the day,' 'He had it coming to him, the scoundrel,' and 'Get off my foot, will you?' filled the vestibule.

"Before I begin, just one question: there aren't any ships' pursers here, are there?"

He paused, squinting at the crowd. When, after a minute, nobody responded, and he heard no flirtatious cries of 'HEE-HAW, HEE-HAW!', he smiled.

"Just as well. My respected colleagues: as you know, for the last four months, ever since Captain Neptune

Flannelbottom Bone was carried away into the night skies of Mexico, we have presumed that Bone, the villainous archaeologist and the most unfinancial Member of the Old Relics Society—"

"He owes the Society more than half a million pounds in overdue Membership fees!" blurted a Member named Esmond Horneplush.

"Shut up, Horneplush, let me get on with it."

"And he owes me a fountain pen," grumbled another Member loudly.

"Yes, yes," Perry said quickly. "But why we're here is—"

"And me a manicure file," remonstrated Hermione Dinkus from her wheelchair.

"Yes, yes. But we're here today—"

"And me one too," added an indignant gentleman with a quivering lip.

"He took eighty-seven of my snail shells, from my prized collection, to throw on people's heads from a great height," shouted Binkie Whiskin, his moustache trembling with rage.

"Yes, well, we've come—"

"And what about all the lavatory paper he used to steal? That was *very* inconvenient!"

Many Members shuddered at this memory.

"Not to mention my bell," said Spong, the Society's Receptionist and Hat-and-Walking-Aid-Checker-Inner. "Heaven knows what he wanted with *that*!"

"He even stole my lipstick once," yelled a large

woman with a boldly coloured artificial fuchsia pinned to her bosom. "The sly cad!"

"I told you to get off my foot!"

"YES, YES, YES!" Perry screamed at the gathering. "Enough!"

The crowd quietened down (except for one man who was starting to mutter something about the unexplained disappearance of the embalmed jackal called Ralph that had been mounted above the salad bar in the Setiteti Bistro upstairs, until the man next to him poked him in the ribs, and he promptly stopped).

"As you have all just shown," Perry said, in a quieter tone, "Neptune Bone was well known to be a thief, a plunderer, and a usurper of all things Right And Meant To Be."

"And lavatory paper!"

"And lavatory paper," Perry added through gritted teeth. "As I was trying to tell you all, up until this point we have presumed him to be dead."

"Up until this point?" whispered Jim to Doris and Brenda. "Does this mean he's still alive?"

Perry went on. "Today, ladies and gentlemen and everyone else, presumption will be laid to rest. For here, I have *proof* that Bone is no more."

The vestibule became silent, waiting for what was to come.

Gerald Perry gestured to two big men, who brought forth a large wooden box and laid it on the top of the reception bureau.

 23

"Jim," Doris prerked, "is Bone inside that?"

"Don't think so. It's too small. He was huge, remember?"

"Huge? He was overblown!"

The big men removed the lid of the box and placed it out of sight.

"My friends," Perry said gravely, "here is all that is left of that scourge to our profession, Neptune Bone."

He rolled up his left sleeve and reached into the box. "You will all know this from its bad taste and clashing of colours."

Slowly he held up a hat: a fez, battered and water-stained, chocolate-brown in colour with a Turkish-delight-coloured tassel.

Many in the gathering shuddered and screwed up their noses. There was no doubt it had belonged to Bone – no one else would ever wear such a brutal combination of hues.

"Rark!" Doris hopped up closer to Jim. "That's the same fez he was wearing the night the Big Wings got him at Uxmal!"*

"So it is," Brenda thought.

"But there's more," said Perry, sounding like a man trying desperately to sell steak knives and sharpening appliances. He put down the fez and beckoned one of the big men. The man lowered his arms into the box.

---

* See *Cairo Jim and the Quest for the Quetzal Queen: A Mayan Tale of Marvels*.

 24

"Let me warn you all," Perry advised, "that some of you might find this other piece a bit gruesome. You may care to turn your heads until it is put away again."

Of course, nobody in the vestibule turned their heads, especially those who were *most* likely to find it gruesome.

Everything was silent, except for the sound of dozens of fat ice-cubes spilling from the box and clattering onto the marble floor. The big man raised his arms and held a revolting object above his head:

The lower half of a human leg!

"This, my friends," said Perry, "is all that we have left of Bone. You will be under no doubts that this is the left lower leg of the man in question. Note the hem of the Crimplene plus-fours trousers that would have once extended to just below the knee. See the coarse stocking, printed with a design of oranges and lemons. And observe, on the foot here, the grubby spat-type shoe, so favoured by the bloated man himself."

Another round of mutterings arose:

"Yes, that leg's Bone's, all right."

"He always had such awful taste in clothing."

"It looks like it's been ripped off the rest of him!"

"You don't see fabric like *that* any more!"

"Yeerrrggghhh."

And, "Look, for the last time, will you get off my foot!"

"The fez, and what's left of Bone, were washed up onto a beach on the island of Samos," Perry announced, gesturing to the man to replace the leg into the

ice-cubed box. "Bone was heinous," Perry told the crowd. "Nobody knows that better than Jim of Cairo, Doris, and Brenda the Wonder Camel, who happen to have joined us this afternoon." He held his arm out in their direction, and all the heads turned. More murmurings swelled:

"There they are!"

"The Society's shining lights!"

"Isn't Brenda looking well?"

"Doris! Hello, you noble bird!"

"Bravo for Mexico, Jim!"

"Jaunty pith helmet – is it new?"

"I wish all our younger Members were like them."

And, "I'm not going to warn you again, GET OFF MY FOOT!"

Perry clapped his hands sharply, and all the heads turned to face him once more. "We shall quietly bury the leg and the fez in our Courtyard of Nothing More in This Realm. No, don't protest; the Board has debated it, and we have decided that no matter how bad Bone was, he was still an archaeologist by profession, and *that* is something we will honour. The profession, not the man."

Most in the assembly nodded quietly in agreement, except for one man who was knocked to the floor by another man who had some very sore toes.

"Now, on behalf of the Old Relics Society, may I invite you to remain here for the afternoon. Have lunch, if you wish, in the Setiteti Bistro, or browse in our extraordinary Library. Or potter about amongst our artefacts in any of our Relics Rooms. Thank you and good afternoon."

There was a soft round of applause, and slowly the crowd began to shuffle off into the great building.

Perry stepped down from the platform and threaded his way through the throng until, after what seemed like a minor, bustling eternity, he was with Jim, Doris and Brenda.

"My friends!" He stroked Brenda's mane (she gave a *quaaaooo*), tousled Doris's crest (she gave a *prerrrk*) and shook Jim's hand (he gave a wide grin). "So glad you showed; I was going to pop out and see you all later today, after I'd attended to this Bone business."

Jim sighed. "It's still hard to believe he's actually gone. He always seemed to be thwarting us at every turn. Now we can all get on with things without the threat of his lurking shadow and those disruptive schemes."

"Mmm. Sometimes the After Life is long overdue." Perry's eyes twinkled. "Found anything at Giza yet?"

"Not a thing, apart from the natural elements of the plateau. We're wondering if you could tell us some more."

"Fill us in," said Doris, "on what we're after."

"Ah!" Perry exclaimed. "The *diary*."

"The diary?"

"The diary? Rark!"

"Quaaoo quaaoo?"

"Oh, yes." Gerald Perry Esquire looked to the right and to the left and, when he was sure nobody was paying them any attention, he lowered his voice to a whisper. "Come with me, into the Library."

3

MUSTY VOLUMES AND
FORGOTTEN THINGS

JIM AND DORIS DISMOUNTED Brenda, and they followed Gerald Perry through the vestibule and into one of the many long, tall corridors that criss-crossed the insides of the Old Relics Society.

"What diary are you talking about?" asked Jim, after a few minutes of walking. Brenda's hoofs echoed as she clip-clopped along the wooden floors.

"Oh, it's good to be back." Perry smiled, ignoring his friend's question. "Those cruises are a pain in the Equator, let me tell you."

Doris perched on Jim's shoulder and said, "Did you go on this one with that French woman again? Mademoiselle Fifi Glusac, the harmonica player and contortionist?"

Perry blushed heavily, coughed a few times into his closed hand, but did not reply.

Presently, after many more echoing minutes, they arrived at the entrance of the Society's Library, a huge cavernous area filled with bookshelves, books, large oak reading tables, potted palm trees, big leather armchairs and bronze statuettes of long-forgotten archaeologists and even longer-forgotten ancient gods and emperors.

Perry stopped directly beneath the marble crest

over the entrance. Carved on this crest was one of the Society's mottos: 'You Never Know When You'll Need a Good Bit of String.'

"Y'know," Perry began, "when I had this place built, way back when the sun shone in an altogether different sort of way, I decided to make this Library the size of three football fields put together. Big! Many of m'colleagues laughed at me – they said that it was too much space, and that I should use all that room for a billiards hall, or an area to have wheelchair races in. But, no, I stuck to m'guns. I've always thought that you can never have too much room for books and quiet contemplation."

"A worthy sentiment." Cairo Jim smiled.

"Now, follow me. There's another thing about having a lot of room like this: you never know when the unexpected will be tucked away somewhere, only to lunge out at you when you're not looking!"

He went into the Library, and the others followed closely.

Cairo Jim took a deep breath. "Musty volumes," he murmured contentedly. "There's no smell quite like it, is there? Sweet and old and full of hints. Someone should invent a fragrance called 'Musty Volumes', to be worn by people who love books and all things Historical."

Doris said nothing, but rolled her small eyes.

There were not many people in here today, despite the fact that it was one of the coolest and quietest places in all of the Society's headquarters. Only a few drowsy old Members were relaxing in the fat armchairs with the morning newspapers, or inspecting the towering bookshelves, looking for a volume that they had remembered reading when they were young archaeologists or explorers, long before they had retired and had grown old.

"Good," whispered Perry. "The place is almost deserted. Makes it better for us." He hunched his shoulders, pressed his fingertips together, raised his elbows, and proceeded to tiptoe in a way he had seen actors tiptoe in certain silent movies, usually in scenes of great secretiveness. "This way, then," he beckoned.

Into the Library he tiptoed, Jim doing likewise and Brenda doing her best to be light and nimble of hoof. Luckily most Members in the Library were well on the deaf side, or didn't have their hearing-aids turned on, so her clacking steps went unnoticed.

Soon, after creeping and fluttering through aisles of forgotten books and darting behind the larger statuary, Perry led them to a far corner of the Library; a corner hemmed in by massive bookshelves and four enormous potted palms, around the base of which sprouted big, thick fern fronds.

"Through here," said Perry, ducking through the narrow gap behind the ferns. Jim, Doris and Brenda copied him (Brenda inhaled deeply, to fit through).

"Coo." Doris blinked. "We're all hidden." She peered out through the fronds, into the rest of the Library. "I bet they don't even know we're here."

Perry went over to a large reading desk, the surface of which was covered in dark green leather. The only object on this desk was a small statue of the ancient jackal-headed god, Anubis. Another, larger, Anubis statue stood on the floor, behind the potted palms and ferns, and in front of the bookshelves at the rear wall.

"I designed this corner for myself," Perry confided, "way back when I had the place built. Put those two bookshelves in there, at those angles, so they looked like the spot where the walls of the Library end. Then I cemented down those pots to camouflage the gap between the bookshelves. Those palms were only about so tall" – he raised his hand to just above his head – "when I planted 'em."

"Perry, it's like a small oasis," said Jim, removing his pith helmet and desert sun-spectacles.

"Quaaooo," snorted Brenda. She moved over to the corner of the oasis and sat down so she could see the titles on the spines of the books there. Maybe there would be some old western adventure novels she hadn't yet read.

"It is indeed a small oasis," said Perry, rubbing his moustache this way and that. "Have a seat, Jim and Doris. Yes, as far as I *knew*, no one else had ever come in here. Only me. It's the perfect place to get away from all the squealing that goes on when the fellows get too excited, and that *does* tend to happen, usually when one of them has chipped a tooth on a chocolate bar or has remembered where he put that stash of pennies he'd collected when he was ten years old. I usually come here on such occasions, or just to read the papers or to plan out how I'd like to have m'hair cut. Nobody can spy me in here, y'see, and that's a good thing, especially when I'm trying to design a new hairstyle for m'self."

"You said as far as you *knew*, no one else had ever come in here," said Jim, sitting in the armchair opposite the desk. "Do you think someone else *has*?"

"Oh, someone else has, yes, someone else has *indeed*! How else d'you think I would've discovered the diary?"

"Rark! Please, tell us what this diary is!"

"I'll do better than that, Doris," Perry said, in a voice that was almost a purr – he was enjoying sharing all this with them. "I'll show you how I discovered it!"

Jim looked at Doris, and she at Jim. Brenda was happy looking at the spines of the books.

"I was sitting here one afternoon," Perry informed them, leaning forward and resting his elbows on the green leather desktop, "a couple of days before that wretched cruise was to sail, as a matter of fact. No sooner had I sat down with a new hairdressing catalogue that'd just arrived from Maurice of Cairo's Coiffure Emporium, than I fell fast asleep!"

Perry paused and pulled a now-that-doesn't-happen-to-me-very-often-I'll-have-you-know sort of face.

"Yes?" said Jim. "Go on."

Perry frowned and continued. "Now that doesn't happen to me very often I'll have you know – I'm usually the last one awake at our late-night slide evenings and things like that. But this particular afternoon was very sleep-making, and before I knew it I was out like a light. I slumped across the desk, like this, with my head down in the little cradle of my arms." He slumped forward to show them, and placed his head in the cradle of his arms, with his face pressed against the desktop.

"Yes?" said Jim. "What happened then?"

"Thphsn, erghvvtphsr ergh csrouplphs ovv herzs, aigh staighrred erghnd woaghke. Erght vvaighrst aigh daighd-n't knoaghw whphsre aigh werghs, oaghn erghcsount ovv mugh vverghcsre beaighng herghrd erghgerghaighnst—"

"Perry, we can't understand a word you're saying."

Gerald Perry lifted his head from the desk and blinked. "I'm sorry. Yes, as I was saying: then, after a couple of hours, I stirred and woke. At first I didn't know where I was, on account of my face being hard against the table. I sat upright again" – he did so – "and stretched my arms, just like this, while I had a bit of a yawn. Look what happened."

He sat back in his chair, while Jim and Doris watched intently. With a stretch and a mock yawn, Perry spread both arms wide on either side of his body, and the fingers on his right hand brushed against the snout of the small statuette of Anubis. "Now, watch the statue closely," he whispered.

One second passed. Then, with no sound at all, the lower jaw of Anubis dropped open.

"Well, swoggle me surreptitiously," muttered Cairo Jim.

"Sh!" shushed Perry. "There's more!"

Behind him, on the bookshelf just above his head, a single volume slid across to the right. *Clack.* On the shelf below that, another book slid to the right – *clack* – and on the shelf below *that*, another did the same. *Clack!* On all the shelves all the way down to the floor a single book slid across the empty space next to it, *clack, clack, clack, clack, clack,* until finally, on the shelf closest to the floor, a book was pushed forward and fell out of the shelves and bumped against the leg of the bigger Anubis statue.

Slowly, with a thin creaking, a small door in the chest of the bigger Anubis swung open. Inside the chest cavity lay a small book bound in violet buckskin.

"Crack my crest," Doris squawked.

"Quaaaooo!" snorted Brenda, who had been watching since the first book had clacked away. She rose and moved to be alongside Jim and Doris.

"I've heard of people wondering if they've got a book in them," commented Jim, "but this is ridiculous."

Perry got up and took the book out of Anubis. "That's exactly what happened when I had my first yawn," he said, sitting down again and laying the small volume on the tabletop. "I checked it all out," he added, gesturing to the bookshelves and the Anubises with his thumb. "She rigged everything up with wires and little pulleys. I guess she wanted someone to find this, if the worst came to the worst, even though she hid it so well."

"She? *She?*" Jim was almost jumping out of his chair with curiosity. "For goodness' sake, Gerald, who *is* she?"

Perry smiled, and turned the book so that it was facing Jim, Doris and Brenda. He pushed it gently across the green leather. "This is who."

The archaeologist-poet leaned forward and read the name that had been printed in lavender ink across the front cover. "Bathsheba Snugg."

"Bathsheba Snugg," repeated Perry.

Jim's head shot up to look at his patron. "It can't be!"

"It can be. In fact, it is."

"Shrink me and glaze me and call me a ushabti! This is incredible!"

"Rerk, what's incredible? What's going on?" Doris flexed her wings impatiently.

Jim ran his fingers delicately around the edges of the book. "The lost diary of Bathsheba Snugg," he said in an awe-filled whisper. "It's been missing for decades!"

"So we thought," Perry nodded. "But not any longer, eh?"

"Bathsheba Snugg? Reerraarrk! Bathsheba Snugg? Who in the name of Dorothy is *she*?"

Jim put his other hand on her wing to settle her. "Not is, my dear, *was*. She was one of the early founding Members of the Old Relics Society, along with Perry here."

"That she was," said Perry, his eyes becoming foggy behind an invisible veil of memory. "Way back, long ago. She was the person, in fact, who convinced me to spend m'money on building the place. A woman of great foresight, she was. Ah!"

"She was one of the most pre-eminent archaeologists at the beginning of the century." Jim had a faraway look on his face. "She was a great scholar, as well, and an expert on the ancient writings of the Greek philosopher and traveller, Herodotitis. She spent much of her life travelling to the same places he did, and recording what had happened to those places, and translating his works."

"She was a dashing figure, to boot," added Perry wistfully. "I often used to—"

"Rark! You used to *kick* her?"

"Eh? Kick her? No, never." Perry's eyes bulged at the suggestion.

"No, my dear," said Jim. "'To boot' is just a figure of speech."

"Rerk."

"I was going to say," Perry went on, "that I used to watch her clambering off over the sand dunes or scampering round the columns of Karnak Temple, or scaling a towering date palm, which she had a tendency to do, all the time in a long black skirt and pointy red boots and a frilly white blouse with a big leather belt that had a dozen pockets slung on it..."

"You used to wear a long black skirt?" Doris slapped a wing across her beak. "And frilly white blouse? And pointy red boots? It's lucky you weren't arrested!"

"No, Doris, he means Bathsheba Snugg used to wear all that."

"Quaaoo." Brenda nudged the book's corner with her left nostril.

"Oh," said the macaw. "So what happened to Bathsheba Snugg, then?"

"Disappeared," said Perry. "About forty years ago. Went off into the desert, and no one heard of her again. I remember seeing her leave the Society here on the very morning of her disappearance ... she was most excited about something she'd just read. Reckoned she knew where there was a very important ancient site out there on the Giza plateau – she told me as much as she hurtled down the front steps, her long, black hair billowing behind her like the clouds of the After Life in hot pursuit." Perry gave another sigh and looked off into the distance.

Jim said, "It was known that she always kept a diary, a record of all her studies, especially of the writings of Herodotitis. But when she vanished, so did the diary. And so did any knowledge of this huge discovery that she claimed was waiting to take place."

"Quaaaooo!" Brenda nudged the diary with her other nostril.

Perry clapped his hands loudly in front of him. "That is, until now! Open it, Jim, go on, to the page I've put m'bookmark into. Read it out loud for us all!"

"Rightio." Jim carefully opened the book at the place marked by Perry's alligator-shaped osnaburg bookmark. "The entry for June third?" he asked.

"Mm-hm," Perry nodded, his eyes wide and glinting like a possum's.

"'June third, 1908. Oh, dearest diary—'"

"Oh, brother!" said Doris.

"Sh, my dear.

'Oh, dearest diary, never in all my wildest

dreams would I have expected to turn up what today came across my vision.

'I was sitting quietly and studiously (as I always do after a strenuous morning of trying to get my hat back from a thieving donkey), translating a new fragment of the works of the great Herodotitis, when the words he had written two and a half thousand years ago leapt out at me with such startling ferocity I almost fell off my stool. The Big H. had been describing the Seven Wonders of the World for nearly sixty lines, raving about the majesty of the monuments and the times that it had taken him to travel to each one, across seas and sands and scrub, when he dropped an antediluvian bombshell.

'Oh, wise and hushed diary, Herodotitis found a greater thing than all of these other Wonders. Here are his exact words, translated by myself this afternoon:

The Temple of Artemis at Ephesus, the Colossus of Rhodes, the Hanging Gardens of Babylon, the Pharos at Alexandria – yea, they are all marvellous. These, and the others of the Seven Wonders, are all unspeakably great. But there is something I have discovered that is far greater; a structure that is more marvellous, more astonishing, more breathtakingly, ambitiously and stunningly built, than all of the Seven Wonders of the World put together. A monument so brilliantly constructed that it defies explanation.

It is to be found in the shadows of the sand dunes one thousand paces due south of Chephren's Pyramid. But tread carefully…Greatness such as this is easily toppled.

'I plan, oh, quiet and secretive diary, to leave first thing in the morning, to discover this, the Greatest of the Greats. How good it will be to get out into the field once more.'"

Jim finished reading and looked up. His face was pale and his cheeks and arms were tingling with a fine layer of goose pimples. "Greater than the Seven Ancient Wonders put together? Perry, this could be bigger than … this could be the biggest thing there ever was!"

"That it could, Jim. Which is why I got you all up here pronto pronto to start digging."

"Quaaaooo," Brenda snorted, noticing that the entry Jim had read aloud was the very last entry in the diary.

"Rark, I'm practically squawkless!"

"So many questions," said Jim, frowning. "What happened to her? Did she find this thing that Herodotitis described? And, most importantly, what in the name of Cleopatra is it that she went after, and that *we're* all looking for?"

"Maybe," Doris suggested, "this Herodotitis fellow wrote some more about it? Maybe we can find the answer in his ancient scrolls?"

"Unfortunately," Perry said, "Bathsheba never identified the *exact* piece of Herodotitis's writing that she was translating on June third, 1908. And, until we find it, we won't know precisely what he was writing about. I've got some of the archivists down there in the Papyrus Rooms going through all the scrolls and fragments, but I don't like our chances; as far as I'm aware, the only person who ever bothered to translate Herodotitis was Bathsheba Snugg. And, apart from this diary, all her translations and papers have been lost. I'd be willing to bet that she took this particular scroll off with her that morning when she went tearing out of here."

Cairo Jim felt a surge pass through his body, all the way up his spine and into his ears, which tingled with the prospect of unimaginable possibility that might be lying in the sands of Giza. "In the shadows of the sand dunes. Hmm. Whatever it is we're after, it's buried out there. And the only way we'll uncover it is to dig and dig and dig."

Doris hopped up onto Brenda's saddle. "Come on then, let's go. The Sphinx will grow its nose back if we stay here much longer!"

"Here, Jim, take the diary with you. Keep it in your tent. We're all in the dark on this one, but having the source of the information in the diary might make it all a little more reassuring while you're searching."

"Thanks, Perry." He took the diary, put it into Brenda's saddlebag, and climbed swiftly up onto the saddle. "Towards Greatness," he said, before turning Brenda to canter noisily off through the Library.

"May all your ibises come home to roost," said Gerald Perry Esquire as he watched them go.

4

BACK TO THE DIG

FOR THE NEXT WEEK, Cairo Jim kept digging.

He, Doris and Brenda would rise early, an hour before the sun, when the air was crisp and cool and the morning was quiet. A quick breakfast of fruit, snails (for Doris, specially flown up from Malawi via Gurna village) and worms (for Brenda), and then the trio would head off from their tent and walk one thousand paces south of Chephren's Pyramid.

Jim continued the hole he had started when they had come up from the Valley of the Kings. Deeper and deeper it got, while Doris and Brenda watched from the sidelines.

He would fling the dirt and sand into a wide pan on the ground above him, and the Wonder Camel would drag the pan, when it was filled, to a dumping mound a few hundred metres from the dig. There she would empty it and bring it back to be refilled. Doris kept a careful eye on the bottom of the hole, ready to squawk if she saw anything being exposed by Jim's shovel.

(She was also waiting for the time when she could do her best work to help Jim: if and when he found something, she was ready to swoop down and begin dusting the object off with her sensitive wingtips. She could work

41

much faster and far more delicately than the finest of archaeological brushes.)

When the sun had passed overhead, Jim would ask Doris what the time was. She would take his pith helmet and hold it up to the sky, in the direction of the east. After squinting through one of the hat's ventilation holes, she would usually announce that it was one o'clock. (Jim was still astonished that she could do this, but she would not reveal how.)

By one o'clock in the afternoon it was too hot to continue working, so they all retired to the tent and the shade of the tarpaulin that Jim had put up for Brenda. Here they rested, while Jim wrote up the results of the morning's work or sometimes dabbled with a poem he was trying to pen. Then, later in the afternoon when the sun was setting behind the pyramids, the trio would return to the hole and dig for another hour or two in the cool of the early evening.

At the end of the week, they had still uncovered nothing except rocks and rubble.

On the eighth morning, Jim stopped and leant on his shovel. "You know something?" he asked Doris and Brenda.

"Rerk. What?"

"Quaaoo. Quaaaoo?"

"Maybe we're going in the wrong direction." He took a long swig from his water bottle as the perspiration trickled down the inside of his shirt.

Doris fluttered into the hole, and stood on the

ground in front of Jim. "What do you mean, the wrong direction?"

"Well," he puffed, "here we are, digging down and down and down. Maybe I should get back up there on the ground and start digging *across*."

Brenda listened, and nodded her head in a wide circle.

"Across?" spluttered the macaw.

"Mm-hm." He took from his shirt pocket a bit of paper on which he'd copied the words from Bathsheba Snugg's diary. "The diary said that whatever this thing is, it can be found 'in the shadows of the sand dunes one thousand paces due south of Chephren's Pyramid'. We're due south here, but 'due south' covers a big area, especially when your point of pacing is something as big as Chephren's Pyramid."

Doris blinked and stretched her wings.

"So," Jim hoisted himself out of the hole, "maybe we should start digging over a broader area but not quite so deep. Maybe what we're looking for will yield a clue nearer to the ground?" He scanned the dunes and the rough, yellowish-brown landscape around them all. "If only what we're searching for could speak to us through all this sand," he wished aloud.

Doris flew up and came to rest on Brenda's fore hump. "Don't worry, Jim of Cairo," she squawked. "We'll find this whatever-it-is, 'even from the tongueless caverns of the earth', as Shakespeare wrote in *Richard II*, Act One, Scene Two. Rark!"

"Very good, Doris."

"Quaaaooo," snorted Brenda.

And so they walked thirty of Jim's paces to the west, and there started to dig again.

Late that afternoon, after they had eaten an early dinner and had come back to their new dig to make the most of the last few hours of gentle sunlight, an unexpected intrusion occurred.

A huge shadow blotted out the sun, and the Giza plateau south of the Pyramid of Chephren was plunged into a great smudge of murkiness.

"What the—?" muttered Jim, stopping with his shovel in the air.

"We're not expecting an eclipse, are we?" spluttered Doris, blinking up into the sky.

Brenda snorted in the negative, and then snorted excitedly as she spied something. She pointed to the pyramids with her hoof.

"What is it, my lovely?" Jim asked her.

"Look!" Doris saw it as well. "Between Chephren's Pyramid and the Great Pyramid of Cheops!"

"Well swoggle me stratospherically!" gasped the archaeologist-poet.

There, in the wide V-shaped space that lay between the two gigantic pyramids, a strange shape was emerging, rising and swelling up as it came over the horizon far behind the magnificent monuments. As it grew bigger, it blocked out more and more of the sun behind it.

A breeze began to pick up, sending the finer grains of

sand whizzing around the tops of the nearby dunes. Brenda hurriedly clamped her nostrils shut in case a sandstorm suddenly developed.

"Jim!" Doris flew to his shoulder. "Is that what I think it is?"

Jim squinted hard through his desert sun-spectacles. "I'd say it is, my dear."

The strange shape rose higher, still covering the sun, and then it stopped for a few moments between the Pyramids. With a clunk, it changed course and slowly started to approach Jim, Doris and Brenda. As it came closer, the end-of-day sunlight began streaming out all around it, and the shadows lifted from the ground.

"There's only one person I know who could handle a montgolfier* like that," Jim smiled.

The green-and-blue striped balloon was directly overhead now, and out over the side of the basket popped a head covered with tangly auburn curls and wearing a large set of flying goggles. "Jim! Doris! Brenda! Like an extra pair of hands for a week?"

"Look, gang, it's Jocelyn!" Jim couldn't stop beaming as he watched his good friend, Chief Stewardess Jocelyn Osgood of Valkyrian Airways Limited, hurl down her anchor. He beamed more broadly as he observed her climbing down the spindly rope ladder she had tossed over the side of the basket.

---

* A large and beautiful hot-air balloon, kept afloat by a small fire from underneath.

 45

"I hope she's not brought any ribbons to tie in my feathers again," Doris prerked with some distaste.

By the time Jocelyn Osgood, Valkyrie of the Skies, had tethered the montgolfier, the sun had all but disappeared, and the warm breezes of the evening were engulfing everything that was on the Giza plateau.

At the campsite Jim lit the kerosene lamps, and he and Jocelyn erected the small tent that Jocelyn had brought for herself. Doris and Brenda set to building the campfire, which was soon burning steadily (the nights quickly changed from warm to cool here, and a fire was necessary).

Then, over glasses of ice-cold water and strong Egyptian tea, and with the montgolfier floating above them like a mighty bubble of aerodynamic silence being buffeted gently by the breeze, they talked and snorted and squawked.

"Yes, Jim," said Jocelyn, "Norway *was* interesting. I had a time of it, and lost a good colleague. But I'll tell you about that later. Let's talk about you and Doris and Brenda, and why you're all here. That's why I've come. I've got a week off between flights, so I hired Persephone" – she gestured above her head to the montgolfier – "to see if I could help you out."

"It's good to get together again, Joss." Jim had combed his hair especially. "Isn't it, gang?"

Brenda rolled her head in the affirmative, but Doris pretended to be interested in her book of Shakespeare's plays opened next to her perch. She had observed, soon after Jocelyn's arrival, the lingering way in which Jocelyn had shaken Jim's hand, and the macaw couldn't get the image out of her mind.

Jocelyn sipped her tea and smiled. "I read in the *Egyptian Gazette* that they found Neptune Bone's leg, washed up on an island. So he *is* gone?"

Jim nodded. "And life's been much more peaceful, too."

"What a senseless waste of a clever brain," Jocelyn said. "When he was younger, he could have done anything with that mind."

Jim stared into the fire. "His is a name to be remembered in the approach of storms, and at other dark and gloomy times."

"You can say that again," Doris squawked. "Especially when there's a lot of wind about, that's when we'll remember Neptune Flannelbottom Bone!" She looked up and saw Jocelyn smiling at her. She quickly dipped her beak and went back to her Shakespeare.

"Yes," Jim went on, "things have been a lot more calm since he went. But frustrating as well. Very frustrating."

"Quaaaooo," agreed Brenda as she sat on her special camp rug.

Jocelyn put down her cup and gave her friend a spill-the-beans-all-over-me look.

For the next ten minutes, Cairo Jim told Jocelyn all

about their dig: why they were digging here; the meeting with Perry; the fact that they didn't know what they were looking for.

"How strange," she said when he had finished.

Jim fished out the bit of paper on which he'd copied Bathsheba Snugg's words, and gave it to Jocelyn, who read it silently.

"One thousand paces," he pondered. "If only Herodotitis had been more specific. If only he'd given us some extra information."

"Jim?" Jocelyn asked in her thoughtful tone. "I know you're a very *exact* sort of archaeologist, and you'd have measured the distance properly and everything—"

"He sure did!" Doris blurted.

"Yes, yes, I'm not doubting, but would you mind very much if I did the pacing for myself?"

The moon had by now risen high – a full moon, bright and glowing like it only gets above the pyramids and the Great Sphinx and the plains and sand dunes of Giza.

"No, of course I wouldn't," answered Jim. "Two pairs of legs can't do any harm, can they?"

Brenda was listening intently, her tail flicking from side to side. She agreed with that last statement whole-heartedly, from a lifetime of personal experience.

"Good." The Flight Attendant stood and handed the paper back. Then she headed off towards the hulking, dark pointed mass of the Pyramid of Chephren.

"Would you like a lighted branch from the fire?" called Jim, placing the bit of paper on his camp stool and reaching for the firewood pile.

"No thanks, there's enough moonlight to almost see my own shadow!"

He and Brenda watched her as she headed back to the base of the Pyramid. She grew smaller and dimmer, her powder-blue jodhpurs glowing against the night sand. Then, after she had reached out and touched the stones in the mighty Pyramid with her determined fingertips, she turned and started pacing back towards Jim, Doris and Brenda.

Jim couldn't take his eyes off her shimmering figure as she came nearer, striding boldly yet gracefully across the small dunes and grittiness underfoot. He gave a sigh, which Doris heard, and the macaw gave a dismissive sort of screech, which Brenda heard, and *she* gave a snort full of joy at being part of this friendship, in this wonderful part of the world.

"Four hundred and seventy-nine," Jocelyn breathed as she strode through the campsite and kept on pacing and counting into the moon-bathed dunes.

After more minutes of pacing, she stopped and put her hands on her hips. "One thousand," she called from the shadows. She looked all around her and saw the rubble from their dig and the wide pan that Brenda used to cart the rubble away from the hole. Further to the west she saw, lit up by the bright shafts of moonlight, the shallower diggings that Jim had commenced more recently.

She nodded her head and came back to camp.

 49

"You're spot on with the pacing," she told him, her curls tangling in the breeze.

"Of course," Doris muttered to herself.

Everything Jocelyn had done had been observed by Brenda, and her eager, Wonder Camel brain had been ticking over throughout. With a thrill of electricity, her mane stood on end as the idea came to her.

While Jim and Jocelyn were talking about the dig, and while Doris was nodding off on her perch but trying to keep one eye open to watch Jim and Jocelyn at the same time (in case any ribbons suddenly appeared from Jocelyn's pockets – amongst other reasons), Brenda quietly rose from her rug and fetched a hefty branch from the pile of firewood.

Then, with the branch clamped between her jaws, she headed off, unseen like the breeze, into the night.

5

MOON-BLAZING INTUITION

WITH EACH HOOFSTEP SHE TOOK, Brenda the Wonder Camel gave a quiet snort as she kept count.

The moonbeams streamed down onto her humps and the tops of the small sand dunes around her, and cast long, shimmering shadows into the sand. Everywhere was quiet out here; she could no longer even hear the muffled chatterings from the campsite. If there had been clouds overhead, she was sure she would be able to hear them gliding across the skies.

As she came to her eight hundredth step, her eyelashes started to tingle with something not natural for a Wonder Camel. Was it the dew of the cooling night? Was it minuscule grains of sand wafting through the air? Or was it the promise of something unknown?

Everyone else had had a go at this thousand paces game, so why shouldn't she? After all, that Herodotitis and that Bathsheba Snugg hadn't written anything about it being a thousand *human* paces…

Cairo Jim couldn't sleep.

He lay on his camp stretcher inside his much-patched tent, staring at the canvas above him and the shape of the moon glowing through it. Since he had

come to bed, he had tossed and turned and turned and tossed. He didn't know whether it was the excitement of Jocelyn's unexpected arrival or the dull, niggling frustration of not being able to find what it was – but not *knowing* what it was – that he, Doris and Brenda were looking for.

This was a night wherein sleep would not come knocking at his door, he decided in his poetic way. So he got up and went to his collapsible card table (which served as his special writing desk while camping) and decided to try and write a poem.

> Here I sit, bereft of sleep
> the thing we're after buried deep
> down in the sandy-studded night
> ouch what is that? An insect bite!

No, it was no good, there were too many distractions to concentrate fully on his art. He screwed up the paper, tossed it onto the dead fire, and decided to go out, into the moon-blazing dunes, and potter about for a bit in the sand.

It was then that he noticed that Brenda was missing.

"Brenda?" he whispered into the darkness (being careful not to wake Doris, who was snoring quietly on her perch by the door-flap to his tent). "Brenda, my lovely? Are you there?"

He waited for her snort, but nothing came. "Brenda?" he whispered again.

The breeze sent a small dusting of sand whizzing across the ground. Jim saw the grains scurrying across the hoofprints.

"Well," he thought as he grabbed the camp's main lantern, "seems like I've got somewhere to go after all!"

After more than half an hour of careful trail following, Jim found her. There against a small dune, her humps snuggled into the sand, Brenda had curled her legs up beneath her and was fast asleep.

Jim went quietly to her and gave her snout a gentle stroke. "You funny Bactrian," he thought. "Sometimes you do the strangest things ... why, you haven't wandered off into the night since you were small and that scoundrel Bone camelnapped you and took you off to Peru."

He sat beside her and breathed in the still desert air that was blowing north from Upper Egypt. The moon was even stronger out here, so far from camp. It was like a small lamp burning right above them.

Then he saw the branch.

The archaeologist-poet stood and went over to it. It was the only bit of wood anywhere out here, and so he reasoned that Brenda must have carried it from camp and stuck it into the sand. But why?

He levered the branch back and forth and dislodged the sand around it. With a small grunt he pulled it free from the ground and looked at it. Puzzled, he dropped it onto the sand.

What happened next made his heart skip five beats.

Cairo Jim's skin erupted in an explosion of goosebumps: goosebumps upon goosebumps upon goosebumps, so many of them he felt like they would rise up over him and devour him.

There had been a sound, when the branch had hit the ground!

When his heartbeat returned to almost normal, and his goosebump invasion retreated a little, he stooped and picked up the branch again.

And again he dropped it.

HOOOMMMPPPPHHHHH. The sound he had heard before.

Jim had been digging these sands and walking on them and putting tents up on them and sometimes dropping his dinner plate on them for the last couple of weeks, and he knew from all that experience that the sands around here did not go HOOOMMMPPPPHHHHH when something struck them.

This HOOOMMMPPPPHHHHH was a new noise, an altogether different sort of sound. His archaeological experience was telling him, like a newspaper headline hurtling through his brain, that the sand here was concealing something more than sand!

One more time, he picked up the branch and dropped it carefully. HOOOMMMPPPPHHHHH!

He sank to his knees and began clearing away the sand with his hands. He swept it to the right and left, his nose pressed close to the ground. He dug it back like a dog preparing a hole for the burial of something important.

And his hands found it: hard and flat, cool and smooth. Big perhaps. It was something, maybe the something they'd been looking for.

Slowly he stood, his spine oscillating with an energy he only ever felt when he was standing on the threshold of unknown discovery. Every pore in his skin was zinging, and his breath was coming in short, shallow gasps.

He looked up at the moon, and suddenly a shaft of bright moonlight hit him in the left eye. He blinked and covered his eyes for a moment. When he took his hands away, the shaft of light had vanished.

Infused with the great possibility that lay beneath him, he dropped to his knees again and feverishly dug away the sand.

6

THE GLINT OF EVIL

"MADE YOU BLINK, YOU DIRTY SKINK!"

Deep within the thick, sweet gloom of the abandoned Whiff of Nefertiti Perfume Parlour, a large, fleshy man lowered his antique telescope from the window and laid it across his countryside of a lap. "I've been trying to glint into your eye for ages. Arrrr!"

Captain Neptune Flannelbottom Bone sat back in his comfy chair and crossed his plump, ball-like ankles on top of a crate that had once contained bottles of Secrets of the Desert fragrance. He took a long drag on his cigar – it was his favourite brand, from the Belch of Brouhaha Tobacco Company – and blew the putrid smoke up into the darkness.

"Ha!" came a raspy voice from the other side of the shop. Desdemona the raven, his flea-infested companion, raised her beak from the half-empty tin of imported Japanese seaweed she had been noisily slurping. Her eyeballs throbbed the colour of blood. "You've been trying to make a glint into the whole world ever since I've known you!"

"And what," Bone seethed, "do you mean by *that*?"

"I mean," she said, pecking a flea from her vent, "that for years you've been trying to make your mark on

the world. You've been going after fame and fortune and food, and you've never got *any*where! Look at us, stuck here in this dump of a perfume parlour, hiding from the Antiquities Squad, and from that stupid statue that comes after you. Sheesh!"

Bone's ginger-brown beard bristled in the cool, empty shop.

"Statues that swoop out of the air. What a world we live in! Craaarrrkkk!"

Slowly Bone reached down and picked up a small perfume decanter that had been left on the floor when the shop's owners had gone. With a swift hurl, he lobbed it at the raven.

"YOOOOUUUUUCCCHHHH!" The decanter bounced off her feathered skull and smashed onto the floor. "Ooh, that hurts worse than the time I sat on that pineapple in Port Moresby." She rubbed the back of her head with her wing.

"Any more of your insults and I'll make sure you become acquainted with more than a *single* pineapple."

"Nevermore, nevermore, nevermore!"

He puffed on the cigar and adjusted his flamingo-coloured fez with the puce-tinted tassel.

"Oooh," moaned the bird. "I don't know why I stay with you. All it ever gets me are bruises and brutal indigestion and eternal running away from the Antiquities Squad."

"Oh, we'll get more than that this time, you fractious framework of frowziness. You don't realise what I've been doing, do you?"

Desdemona stopped rubbing her skull and squinted at him. "Blowing off more hot air?" she rasped.

"Enough!" he hissed.

She cowered into the corner, her deep black feathers blending into the gloom.

"If you'd care to listen, I'll divulge some of my latest Plan of Brilliance to you. Although you don't deserve to bear witness to this, my new Scheme of Genius. Arrrr."

"Go on, my Captain," she said. "Fill me with wonder!"

"I'll fill you with my boot if you don't listen respectfully!"

"All right, all right, all right. I'll be respectful." She folded her tatty wings across her pot-belly and looked up at him as though the moon shone out of his fez.

"That's better." He pulled his emerald-green waistcoat down over his huge stomach and stared out through the dusty window as he puffed on the cigar. "What I have been doing, ever since we evaded the clutches of that dreadful flying thing from Greece, is reconstructing myself."

"Reconstructing yourself? Well, it's about time, if you ask me."

"Enshut your beak!"

"It's enshutted."

The smoke curled up into his beard and moustache and lingered above his fez. "Do you remember, when we were holed up on the island of Samos after our little excursion to Mexico, the big blob of whale blubber that washed up onto the beach?"

"Yeeerrgghh," Desdemona shuddered. "How could I ever forget it? You made me cut it up with my beak and shape it into a big mass of gooiness." Her rough, yellow tongue was hanging out at the sickening thought of it. "I don't know what you wanted with such a thing. I still can't get the taste of it out of my mouth, not to mention all those little hairs that were in it! Bleccchhh!"

"It became part of me," Bone said.

"What?" Desdemona's eyes were wide. "How revolting!"

"I clothed it with part of my plus-fours trousers and with my left spat and stocking. It became part of me, and of my plan to reconstruct myself and the rest of my glorious, dazzling life."

The raven quietened, and readied herself for the rest of his story. "I don't understand," she said.

"That bit of whale blubber, thus attired, looked exactly like my leg. Which is just what I wanted. You see, Desdemona, once it was completed, I left it on the beach, along with one of my many fezzes, and made an anonymous phone call to the Old Relics Society. One of the Society's Greek Members came pronto pronto and collected the pieces and brought them back to the Society here in Cairo. And thus it is that I am believed to be dead. Just as I had planned."

"Well pluck me selectively and call me a kewpie doll," gasped the raven. "Everyone thinks you've carked it!"

"Arrrr. But reports of my death, as the saying goes, are *greatly exaggerated*."

"Just like your stomach," thought the bird, but she said nothing.

"And I plan to make the most of this great exaggeration." He blew a shaft of smoke towards the moon; the smoke exploded silently against the grubby window pane. "The world believes I am dead, and that's the way it will be. Henceforth, Desdemona, the magnificent being known as Neptune Bone will no longer exist. No, from here on in there will be *another* to take his place, another man who shall take the world by storm with his sheer Genius."

"Who? Who's it gonna be?"

"Me, you moron."

"You? I don't get it."

"Me in a different guise. And because the world will not know me in my *new* guise, the world will be astounded by my brilliance in ways it never was when I was Neptune Bone. Furthermore, because no one else *except* Bone has displayed the same sort of brilliance, and because Neptune Bone is 'dead', no one will put me and me together. Arrrr."

"Hmm," Desdemona hopped a few steps closer to him. "Very ingenious."

"Of course it's very ingenious. What else did you expect from someone of my great, everlasting, forward-reaching vision?"

He stretched out his arms, put his hands behind his neck, locked his fingers together and cracked his knuckles loudly (Desdemona's eyes throbbed harder at the noise – it always made her squeamish). "This way," he purred, "I shall be able to start over again, with all my brilliance intact, and without the infernal bother of the Antiquities Squad always on our tails."

"The Antiquities Squad's worse than these fleas, the way it always follows us round," Desdemona muttered darkly.

"Arrr." Bone picked up the telescope again and looked out across the sand dunes.

"I only have one small question."

"And what might that be, you ostinato of odiousness?"

"Why have we been stuck here in this dump of a perfume parlour for the past two weeks? Why don't we just go on out and be brilliant in your new guise, and start to accumulate some wealth and some more tins of Japanese seaweed? My supplies are running low."

"We're watching," answered Bone, squinting through the telescope. "We're going to make some sort of discovery very soon, hopefully the sort of discovery that will make the archaeological world squirm and jump about with excitement."

"What poppycock dost thou spout?" She looked up at him as though he were a bit of the whale blubber she had been so yuckily acquainted with. "How in the name of Hecuba can we make any discoveries stuck here in the Whiff of Nefertiti Perfume Parlour? Sheesh again!"

Bone's flabby lips curled into a smarmy grin. "We're going to discover what that goody-two-boots archaeologist is looking for."

"Jim?"

"Arrrr. The thorn in my paw, the ache in my tooth, the pain in my nether regions, Jim of Cairo."

"And that gaudy, smartie-claws macaw, Doris. Ooh!"

"He's after something out there."

"What? What's he after?"

"That is a question to which I am still seeking an answer. Knowing him, though, it'll be something that he considers to be important. Something that matters to this stinking garbage heap we call 'the world'."

Desdemona hopped up onto the arm of Bone's comfy chair, and pecked a flea from her underwing. "Can you see him?"

Bone adjusted the focus on the telescope. "Hmmm. Yes, for some strange reason he's out there in the dunes. Normally at this hour he's tucked up, safe and goody-goody sound, in his pathetic little tent. Tonight, though, he's a lot further away from where he and his friends have been digging these past few weeks."

"What's he doing out there?"

"Can't tell. He's down on his hands and knees. Looks like he's sweeping the sand with his hands, but I can't quite see; his gluteus maximus is unfortunately pointed in our general direction."

"Maybe he's gone sleep-walking? Or sleep-sweeping?"

"It's very strange. And there, over to the right, is that wretched camel of his. Her eyes are shut tight. She seems to be fast asleep."

"Maybe she's dead, and he's digging a grave for her," Desdemona suggested eagerly. "Ha-crack-har-crack-ha!"

"No, you horrendous hunk of hopefulness, she's not dead. Her nostrils are flaring in and out. She's breathing, all right."

"Ratso!"

Bone moved his telescopic gaze back towards the campsite. "Let's just see if there's any clue we can find amongst all their stupid little belongings. It's making me itch worse than a pair of osnaburg underpants... Hello!"

"Hello," said Desdemona. "How do you do?"

"No, amoeba-brain, I wasn't greeting you, I was making a slightly startled observation. There's an enormous montgolfier tethered above their camp."

"Has it brought its mont*caddy* with it?"

Bone swiped at her with his fat arm, and she fluttered off the chair and onto an empty crate.

"This is not the time for idiocy, seaweed-breath. Hmmm. I wonder who brought *that* in?"

He moved his gaze down, past the montgolfier to the ground, and spied around the camp. "And there's an extra tent as well. Most odd. Hello!"

"Guten tag," said the bird, jumping well out of reach of his foot.

"There," he whispered, his breath short and puffy, his cheeks glistening with the faintest dew of perspiration, "on the sand near the macaw's perch."

"What? What is it?"

"A piece of paper."

"A piece of paper?"

"Arrrr."

"Is that all?"

"A piece of paper *that wasn't there this afternoon.*
He's very neat about his campsite, is Cairo Jim. He'd
never leave a piece of paper on the ground like that.
It's against all his wholesome principles."

"He's dropped it then?"

"Someone has."

"How careless."

He closed the telescope with a loud SNAP and fixed
Desdemona with a commanding stare. "Fly over there,
my feathered fiend, and fetch that piece of paper. Be
careful to avoid the brightest beams of moonlight, and
keep your beak low."

"Aye aye, my Captain." She hopped off the crate
and towards another window that had long ago been
shattered. "It's as good as got!"

With a hop, skip and an unfortunate noise that came
from somewhere deep within her, she disappeared
through the broken glass and became nothing more
than a smudge against the gloom of the night.

"Who knows, it might just lead us closer to the
great discovery that Cairo Jim is preparing for us."
He opened the telescope again and raised it to his
plump eyeball, scanning the sky until he sighted

a flickering of feathery murkiness against the moon.

"Arr," he murmured, following her course. "To the camp, to the camp, you monstrous messenger of mine."

Desdemona's feathery murkiness soared silently across the night, accelerating through the bright beams of moonlight and coasting through the gloom. Bone watched as she suddenly nose-dived down to Cairo Jim's campsite.

"That's it, that's it ... the paper ... BINGO!"

Like a knife slicing through the air, the raven shot down, snapped up the piece of paper in her beak, and shot up again, leaving not so much as a grain of sand disturbed.

In little more than a few heartbeats, she had swooped back through the broken window of the perfume parlour.

"Crark. Here 'tis, Your Scheminus."

Without a word, Bone shut the telescope, reached down and took the paper from her beak. His eyes sleered across the page, becoming bigger and more excited by the second. Then he threw back his head, clenched his cigar between his teeth, and laughed like a gurgling drain that was emptying into an ocean of deep, bottomless cruelty.

"*HA HA HA HA HA HA HA HA HA HAAAAAAAAAARRRRRRRRRRRR!*"

Part Two:

DISCOVERY AND DESERTION

7

GETTING TO THE
BOTTOM OF THINGS

"*PREEERRRRAAAARRRRRRKKK!*" Doris woke with a screech.

(She had been having a dream about an octopus called Octopus Rex, who was the King of All Octopuses until he got into an unfortunate tangle with his mother and started having trouble with his eyes – it was a very strange sort of dream, and Doris was glad to be awakened from it.)

She blinked the sleep out of her eyes, and flexed herself up and down on her perch a couple of times. Then the feathers around her beak bristled.

Feeling something on her left leg, she gave it a shake. In the moonlight she saw a glossy pink ribbon tied delicately above her claw.

"Oh, for squawking out loud," she cried. Down went her beak, and, with a few frantic tugs, she pulled off the ribbon and spat it onto the sand. "That Flight Attendant! The sooner she flies off again in her big bag of hot air, the better!"

Then she noticed that the lamp was still burning inside Cairo Jim's tent. Deciding to see why he was still awake, she fluttered into the canvas structure.

"Jim? How come you're still – *Jim?*"

She blinked again, this time at the tent devoid of her best human friend.

"That's odd," she thought. "He's gone wandering. He hasn't gone off wandering in the night for three years, not since he had that strange bout of sleep-fox-trotting. Brenda and I had to tie him down firmly to his camp stretcher and hide his dancing shoes until it'd all passed. I hope it hasn't come back!"

She hop-fluttered out of the tent and saw at once that the main lantern, which normally hung on a pole in the centre of the campsite, was gone. "Aha!" She was glad that he'd taken this lamp with him – it proved that he hadn't relapsed into another bout of sleep-foxtrotting, which he had always undertaken in the dark, without lanterns.

Doris soared up to the top of Cairo Jim's tent and peered out across the sandhills. The sun was starting to rise from far across the Middle East; a great, faint band of pinkish light was beginning to seep towards the city of Cairo and the surrounding desert.

Then her eyes found what they were looking for: nestled between the still, shadowy sandhills was a faint glow. Doris recognised the colour of the amber glow as belonging to the campsite's centre lantern.

She raised her wings, shook her feathers, and soared silently towards the light.

Jim was down on all fours when she swooped in to land at his elbow.

"Rark, well it's a fine thing you wandering off like

that without telling a bird where you're going!"

He jerked his head up, startled at her sudden appearance. "Doris! My dear, I'm sorry. I came looking for Brenda. She wandered off first."

The Wonder Camel was still sitting with her humps snuggled into the small dune, and was snoozing gently in the morning half-light.

Doris flexed herself up and down. "What's got into her? What's she—?"

"See what she led me to, Doris!" Jim ran his hands over the thing he had been uncovering in the sand.

Doris watched as his fingertips moved excitedly across the surface of this thing – a thing the likes of which she had never seen out here.

"Look, Doris. Look at its smoothness, look at its flatness. Perfectly flat, so finely chiselled. Look how it glints in the disappearing moonlight, and how its colour changes with the coming of the sun!"

"Perm my plumes!"

"I've been walking all around here, my dear, for the last hour or so, dropping rocks onto the sand. Going by the sounds I've been hearing when the rocks have hit the ground, I have a hunch that this here isn't the only one of these we're going to uncover." His voice wavered with the rich thrill of uncertainty.

"What do you think it comes from, Jim? What is it part of?"

He stopped rubbing his hands over the thing beneath him, and kneeled before her. "For the moment, I've no idea. Not the foggiest. But we're surely going to spend the next few days trying to find out!"

For a full day they paced and dropped small rocks onto the sands. Every time they heard the telltale HOOOOMMMPPPPPHHHHH sound, Brenda the Wonder Camel would stick small flags into the ground, at the exact location of the sound. (The flags were made from twigs from the nearby eucalyptus trees, with pieces of ribbon – provided generously by Jocelyn – tied to the tops.)

Soon there were thousands of small flags blowing in the breeze.

"Right," announced Jim, when he felt that there were no more HOOOOMMMPPPPPHHHHHing patches of sand in the vicinity. "Let's start clearing."

He, Jocelyn and Doris set to work, shoulder to wing to shoulder, brushing away the sand. Jim and Jocelyn used two of Jim's All Will Be Revealed By The Passing Of Time archaeology brushes (with the indestructible bristles – guaranteed for many lifetimes), while Doris used the sensitive feathertips of her wings (which could sense an object in the most perceptive of ways).

Brenda took up a shovel in her mouth and scooped up the sand they were clearing and put it into her wide pan. All of this she emptied at the eastern perimeter of the dig.

Gradually, as the days passed, and as the tourist

coaches and buses trundled across the sealed roads far away, an extraordinary thing was being uncovered.

"Arrrr! Drat that camel!"

The large, fleshy man put down his telescope and gave a grimace so sour that if Desdemona had been a bucket of cream, she would have curdled.

"What's wrong? What's she doing now?"

Bone turned his head and exhaled his cigar smoke straight into Desdemona's eyes. "She's dumping all that sand they're clearing away, right in my line of vision. For the last four days, the pile has been growing higher and higher. Like your smell."

"There's nothing wrong with my natural perfume," Desdemona protested, her eyeballs throbbing redly. "Oh, this place is gloomy! When can we go out into the big wide world again and get up to some real mischief?"

"Enshut your beak, you gormless gruesome glob of grunge. You've given me an idea."

"What?" The raven hopped up onto the armrest of his comfy chair, while he leaned over and started rummaging around inside his travelling-trunk. "What's the idea?"

"There *is* a way I shall be able to see what those goody-goody-gumboots are finding out there," came his muffled voice, his oversized bottom squirming on the chair. He lifted his head from the trunk. "Here, Desdemona, take this Polaroid camera and fly overhead. Snap me a photo of their discovery."

"Eh?" She looked at the camera as though it was a bit of rancid seaweed. "And just where do you suppose I can hold that thing while I'm flying? These wings are a vital part of my aero-thermal-dynamicness. I can't fly and hold onto a stupid—"

"You have claws, don't you?" Bone sneered.

She raised first one and then the other. "Oh, how observant you are! How clever of you! You should get a Nobble Prize for your powers of observation!"

He ashed his cigar onto the top of her skull.

"Aaaaarrrrrggggghhhh! Do it again, do it again! You killed at least sixty fleas that time!"

"All you have to do, numbskullfeathers, is to hold the camera between your claws. Then, when you're hovering over the dig, use one of those talons of yours to press the shutter button. That's it there – the red button that's slightly raised."

"Oh." Desdemona squinted at the red button. "Where's the focus?"

"It's fully automatic. It'll focus on any object, no matter how near or far away, by itself. Get me a wide shot of the area; judging from all that sand they're piling up out there, this thing they're finding is pretty big."

"Takes something big to know something big."

"ENSHUT IT!" Bone puffed impatiently on the cigar. "Now go, fly, take OFF into the ozone. Don't let them see you, and bring me back a photograph that will help me plan my Brilliant Procession of Sabotage."

"As good as done." She grabbed the camera and

hopped up to the shattered window. Wriggling her feathered backside carefully, she disappeared through it and into the sky.

Bone leaned back in the chair and took the piece of paper from the pocket of his plus-fours trousers. "Arrr," he murmured as he re-read what Cairo Jim had copied from Bathsheba Snugg's diary.

He muttered the words quietly to himself, turning them over in his mouth as if they were juicy morsels of food which he wanted to savour before he swallowed them. "'Something ... far greater ... a structure ... more marvellous, more astonishing, more breathtakingly, ambitiously and stunningly built than all of the Seven Wonders put together. A monument so brilliantly constructed that it defies explanation.' Arrrr."

He blew out a thick column of smoke and put the paper back in his pocket. Soon, he thought, he would be able to claim this discovery, and with it, he would be able to go forth into the world once again, to clear his name and to re-establish his reputation as a Man of Pure and Unashamed Genius.

And, at that moment, an idea came to him: an idea based upon the words he had just read; an idea so clever, so *unthinkably bold*, that he would be able to redeem his reputation in such a way that no one would ever remember that he had done the skulduggerous things of which he had been accused.

Why, only once in the written history of the world had such a thing as he was planning ever taken place!

 73

He smirked – a wide, excited, gloating smirk that would have kept growing bigger and wider had not Desdemona swooped in through the window.

"Crark! Here 'tis, my Captain. Got good and proper!"

She perched on the edge of the trunk, and he leaned forward and took the camera from her claws. The photo she had taken was hanging from the front of the camera.

"Arrr," Bone grunted. He pulled out the photo and looked at the whiteness. "In just a few seconds this image will be revealed. Did you get an eyeful of what they were uncovering?"

"Nope." She bit a flea off her belly and spat it onto the threadbare carpet.

"No?"

"Too glary out there to see anything. I don't know why it was so glary. The sand seemed to be white, not yellowy-brown like it usually is. The sun was shining on it. Almost blinding me."

"Hmmm. Well, I hope *this* won't be glary. Hopefully it'll shed a bit of *un*glary light on... Look, Desdemona, here comes the image!"

She jumped up onto his spongey shoulder and together they watched the small square of photographic paper. Slowly an image was appearing, creeping into view, getting stronger and clearer by the second.

"What is it?" croaked the raven.

"Give it a moment more."

Before their eyes – his small and scheming, hers red and throbbing – the picture emerged.

"It's done," Desdemona rasped. She squinted at it. "What is it?"

Bone brought it closer to his eyes, then moved it away again. "Arrr."

Desdemona looked confused.

He tilted the picture around so it was on its side, and blinked heavily. "Arrrr."

Desdemona looked more confused.

He held it upside-down and puffed uncertainly on his cigar. "Arrrrr."

Desdemona looked highly confused.

He turned the picture right-way up, put his head to one side, and scratched his beard. "Arrrrrr."

Desdemona looked like the Queen of Confusion.

Then suddenly Bone saw what it was, and his temples turned scarlet with rage. "Desdemona!"

"What? What, what, what, what, what?"

"You blithering bundle of bunglingness! You've botched it!"

"Eh? How?"

Bone's nose crinkled as he held the photo away from his gaze. "You had the camera the wrong way around. It wasn't pointing down, it was pointing *up*. At your—"

Now she saw what she had snapped. "Oh, for the love of – that's my—"

"Yeeerrrggghhhh," shuddered Bone.

Desdemona blushed so hard her feathers got hot. She snatched the photo from his pudgy fingers.

"Bet you've never seen *that* before," Bone said.

"No, and you're never going to see it again!" In a blurred flurry of pecking and clawing, she tore the photo into a hundred tiny pieces and spat them onto the floor. "How embarrassing!"

"You stupid flying slug!" Bone hit her with his fez. "It seems the only way I shall find out what's going on out there is to go out there myself." He stood and faced the window. "It is time," he announced importantly, "to bring forth Mr Impluvium!"

8

VISIONS ALOFT

"WELL," SAID GERALD PERRY ESQUIRE as he stepped from his vintage Bentley and bustled into the campsite, "what is it you want so desperately to show me?"

Jim sprang from his fold-up camp chair and, in three big steps, bounded across to his benefactor and patron. "Thanks for coming," he said, shaking Perry's hand vigorously. "It's time at last!"

"Steady on, Jim, you'll have me going all wonky if you keep on pumping like that."

Jim let go of Perry's hand. "I'm just so full of this excited energy, that's all. I can't seem to settle down."

"Rark," rarked Doris, flying in to land on top of Jim's pith helmet. "That's for sure. His brain's been 'more busy than the labouring spider', as Mr Shakespeare wrote. He's been dying to show you what we've found."

Gerald Perry reached up and patted her crest. "I'm fairly dying to see it, Doris," he smiled. His old, possum-like eyes twinkled with anticipation. "Where's Brenda?"

"You'll find out soon enough," Jim said. "Won't he, my dear?"

"Too right," Doris squawked. "I'd better go off and

join her. Get everything just right for the big unveiling."

"Rightio." Jim raised his arm and bent it, and the beautiful macaw stepped down onto his elbow. "I'll give you the signal from above," he told her.

"Three glints and we show everything," Doris reaffirmed. "See you soon."

Jim jerked his arm gently, and Doris speared up and off to the south.

"This is all very mysterious," said Perry.

Jim smiled. "Come on, let's fling a bit of the mystery to the winds!"

He led the older man a short distance back towards the Pyramids.

"But Jim, I thought you were digging in *that* direction, not... Oh, stick a trout in m'pocket and call me squishy, it's a montgolfier! Haven't been up in one of these since Bunny Curnow lost her earrings down in Aswan in '28."

A blast of flame came from the burner inside the basket.

"And, whacko m'diddlio, if it isn't Jocelyn Osgood!"

Jocelyn waved. "Morning, Mr Perry!"

Perry winked at Jim. "Y'never mentioned that Joss had dropped in," he whispered in his you-secretive-archaeologist-you voice.

"She's been helping us," Jim said, going a bit red. "We've been grateful for the extra pair of hands."

Perry wiggled his eyebrows. "It's nice to have a 'good friend', isn't it?"

Luckily they had reached the basket, and Jim didn't have to continue this line of conversation. "Right," he beamed. "Are we ready?"

"Persephone's never been readier," Jocelyn called over the hissing of the burner. The huge balloon swayed above her. "All in!"

After a few minutes of Perry getting his pants stuck on a bit of wicker of the balloon's basket, and Jim trying to free him, and Jocelyn flaring the flame as the men got further caught up, and the pants tearing loudly in an unfortunate place, and Perry saying in the end that it didn't really matter about these pants anyway, they were never a good fit and always made him look like he had three hips, they were finally ready to lift off.

Jocelyn and Jim untethered the basket, and soon the green-and-blue striped balloon lifted them off the ground.

A steady breeze blew them smoothly past the Great Sphinx and in the direction of the dig. As they came closer, Perry leaned over the side of the basket and craned his neck downwards. "What is it I'm looking for?" he called to Jim.

"Only a few more moments," Jim called back.

Jocelyn pulled some levers attached to the balloon, and the aircraft skirted some low dunes before gliding up between them.

Then Perry let out a startled squeal. "Erk," he said, quickly putting on his desert sun-spectacles. "Talk about glary! Good gracious, Jim, I've never known the Giza plateau to be this white in the sun."

"It's not the Giza plateau," explained Jim. "No, what's so blinding down there isn't sand. It's calico."

"Calico?" Perry asked, confused.

"Five hectares of it," Jocelyn yelled, flaring the burner and turning it down a bit so that the montgolfier descended slightly. "The size of nearly nine football fields. We ordered it from Cairo to protect the discovery."

"We didn't want any sightseers or tourists walking all over it," Jim added. "Not that any'd probably venture this far away from the Pyramids and the Sphinx, but you never know."

Perry stopped leaning and turned to face Cairo Jim. "Now, look, m'friend, I didn't come out here to have an airborne stickybeak at five hectares of calico. I mean t'say, it's very nice and all, but I've been spending a lot of money funding this dig of yours – all those tools and supplies for you and worms for Brenda and Malawian snails for Doris. I didn't think you'd spend m'money on calico. I'm more of an osnaburg man, m'self."

Jim and Jocelyn smiled at each other.

"Why're you two smiling at each other?"

"Watch," said Jim.

He took from the pocket of his shirt his Reflect Upon the Past Archaeological Pocket-Mirror and aimed it at the sun. Quickly he caught the light, and flashed the glint from the mirror three times towards the calico below.

Beneath the montgolfier, Doris and Brenda, positioned at opposite corners at one end of the vast blanket of calico, saw the three glints. "Reerraarrk," Doris screeched to Brenda. "That's the cue, Bren. Let's pull this thing back!"

She took her corner in her beak, and the Wonder Camel took her corner in her snout. Then, keeping their eyes on each other across the wide plain of calico, they both moved slowly backwards at the same time – Doris carefully flying, and Brenda steadily walking.

The calico spread back with them, like an enormous white wave flowing silently out to a desert sea.

At last it was done. The entire plain of calico had been folded back by the macaw and Wonder Camel, and lay in a huge pile at the far end of the discovery.

Above, the eyeballs of Gerald Perry Esquire were for once wide open. So was his jaw, as he stared, startled beyond belief, at the enormity of what was revealed below.

"This is what I think Bathsheba Snugg was referring to when she recorded this thing that 'defies explanation'," said Jim.

Stretching away to all four points of the compass lay a perfectly smooth, perfectly flat floor of limestone slabs. There was not so much as a bump or blemish anywhere on the entire surface.

"Limestone," Jim told the dumbfounded Perry.

"Blocks and blocks of limestone. There're 200,000 – all of them so finely chiselled they might have been carved yesterday."

"But they weren't," chipped in Jocelyn. "Jim's carbon-dated the insect specimens that Doris found between the slabs. Some of the specimens are nearly four and a half thousand years old!"

Perry looked at Jim, then at Jocelyn (as she kept the montgolfier hovering steadily), then back to the limestone slabs. Still he said nothing.

"You can't see the joins from up here," said Jim, "but each block of limestone abuts the next so closely that you can't even get the blade of a penknife between them. Only Doris's feathertips."

At last Perry spoke. "Blow me over with a trombone! It's almost *indescribably* huge! Oh, heavens above, I haven't been this excited since old Binkie Whiskin got his nose stuck in the water cooler on the train to Alexandria!"

Jocelyn Osgood beamed at her good friend, Jim of Cairo. At that moment her proud radiance rivalled that of the sun.

Down on the ground, Doris flew to Brenda and landed on her fore hump. "I bet Perry's excited," she squawked.

"I bet he's positively beside himself," Brenda thought.

"I bet he's positively beside himself," Doris added.

She watched as Jocelyn kept the montgolfier level. "Hmph. I don't need a bag of hot air over *my* head to keep me airborne. Jocelyn is a pretender of the air, Bren, not a natural flying machine like me!"

"Quaaaooo!" Brenda rolled her head in a big circle.

"But why was this floor of limestone blocks laid here?" Perry asked Jim. "What was it part of?"

"Now *that*," Jim smiled, "is something I'm not entirely sure of. But I do know *something* about it. Last night, when I couldn't sleep, I wandered out to it by myself. I discovered something extra down there – something that ... oh, it's better if we go down. We'll tether the balloon back at the campsite, and return on foot. Then I can *show* you."

Jocelyn looked surprised – Jim hadn't mentioned any new discovery to her. Swiftly, she steered the montgolfier back away from the floor of slabs. With no further ado they descended, and quickly landed by the campsite.

"Arrr," Bone sneered, hurling the telescope into his trunk. "There's only one person I know who could handle a montgolfier like that."

"Who?" rasped Desdemona.

"It appears that Cairo Jim has got his 'good friend' Jocelyn Osgood in on the act." Bone's beard bristled.

"Jocelyn Odgoose, eh? The Flight Attendant you used to be so very keen on, yes?"

Bone ignored the raven and started to rummage inside his trunk.

"In the days," Desdemona went on, "when you and Cairo Jim used to be so chummy-chummy? When you used to work on digs together? When you were much, much younger, and much, much slimmer, and much, much—"

"Enshut your seaweed-hole," came Bone's muffled voice.

"Jocelyn Odgoose, Jocelyn Odgoose, Jocelyn Odgoose," taunted the bird.

Bone rose from the trunk and fixed her with a stare that would have turned her to stone, had she been a human and he a gorgon. "You disgusting, drivelling dirtbag. Mention her name no more!"

"Whose name? Jocelyn Odgoose's?"

"Arrrrrr!" He went to grab her by her throat, but she jumped speedily away.

With a great rippling of flesh, he began to wobble with fury: first his stomach, in a tidal wave of blubber under his paisley-swirled shirt and emerald-green waist-coat; then his fatty thighs and flabby underarms, and finally his many chins behind his well-trimmed beard.

"My, what lovely auburn curls *Jocelyn Odgoose* has," Desdemona croaked. "How tall *Jocelyn Odgoose* is, how gracefully *Jocelyn Odgoose* moves in those—"

"Enshut it, raven!" He swiped at her, and again she hopped clear.

"In those—"

"Pipe down!" He threw a broken perfume bottle at her, but she skilfully ducked it.

"In those – wait for it ... JODHPURS! What a dreadful thing is luuurrrrvvve," she rasped. And then, just for fun, she cartwheeled across the threadbare carpet and cried, "Jocelyn Odgoose, Jocelyn Odgoose, Jocelyn Odgoose! Hahahahahahahahaha!"

Bone took a deep breath, and his wobbling subsided. "I have greater things to do than be tormented by a fleabag like yourself. My immediate moments will now be spent on the subtle yet grandiose scheme of things. Anyway, I was never in love with *anyone*."

"And I'm Imelda Marcos."

Bone found what he was after: a black bowler hat that he had bought while passing through Tanganyika many years earlier. He removed his fez and put the bowler onto his greasy hair, as though he was a king and the rounded hat was his coronation crown. "Behold the birth of Mr Impluvium," he muttered breathlessly.

Desdemona forgot all about saying "Jocelyn Odgoose" again, and stared at Bone. "*Impluvium?* What nonsense dost thou spout?"

"I spout no nonsense, slagbeak. I only speak with wisdom. In a few moments, Captain Neptune Flannelbottom Bone will be no more. For a short time, at least. Mr Impluvium will go forth into the world and, with the aid of Jim's discovery out there, Mr Impluvium will restore the name of Bone, and resurrect my incredible Genius. And then the time will be right for me, at last, to 'rise from the dead'."

"What?" The raven wasn't sure if he had toppled into the chasm of madness she had thought he would finally fall into, or if he was indeed speaking of a clever plan that would accomplish what he had said. "Just how do you intend to do all this?"

"First things first," said the fleshy man, delving once again into the trunk. "I shall now shave off my beard and moustache, in order to help my disguise and my transformation into Mr Impluvium. People know my face far too well ... a clean visage will be unrecognisable as Bone."

Desdemona watched as he found his razor kit in its ocelot-trimmed case.

"And then I only need to find a tasteful galabiyya* to wear over my clothes, and the effect will be complete."

"Maybe there's a circus in town with a spare Big Top tent. That's about the only thing that'd fit *you*."

"How miserable your life will be when I am powerful once again."

"Nevermore, nevermore, nevermore!"

"Now, quickly, go and fetch some water for my shave. We have much to do if I am to walk amongst Cairo Jim's diggings this evening!"

---

* A long, flowing cotton garment traditionally worn in Egypt.

△△△△△ 9 △△△△△

A WHAT-NE-WHAT?

"QUAAAOOO," snorted Brenda as she watched Jim, Jocelyn and Gerald Perry walking carefully across the limestone slabs.

"At last," flapped Doris. "I thought the Sphinx would have Sphinxettes before they got here."

"Incredible," Perry was saying as they approached Doris and Brenda. "I can't believe how perfect they are."

"Thank you," said Doris. "We groomed ourselves especially for your visit, didn't we, Bren?"

"Quaaoo."

"Perry means the slabs," Jim said to her. "Not you two."

"No," Jocelyn added, leaning down and picking Doris up. "Your perfection goes without saying."

"Hmph." The macaw fluttered from her hands and landed on Jim's shoulder.

Brenda flickered her long eyelashes modestly.

"They're all so smooth and precise," Perry said, scanning the vast spread of the stones through his desert sun-spectacles. "It's like some great, clean floor."

"That it is," Jim agreed. "That's what I've been thinking since we uncovered the majority of it. A huge floor. But what it was the floor *of*, I had no idea. Have a look around – all around."

Perry, Jocelyn, Doris and Brenda did so.

"See, all there is are slabs. There's nothing else visible. No traces at all of any building foundations or columns. No vestiges of crumbled walls ... there's not an ancient brick to be found!"

"Odd," said Perry. "Most odd."

"Too right it's odd." Jim frowned. "Normally on an archaeological dig – at least on all the ones I've worked on – if you find traces of an ancient floor, you also find bits of walls, or stairwells, or household objects like jars or tools or mummified budgies. But here, all we've got is the one huge floor area."

"We haven't even unearthed any other rock or wood or metal fragments," squawked Doris.

"So the question that niggles," Jim said, stroking Doris's wing thoughtfully, "is: what was the structure that once rose above this floor?"

"And what happened to it?" asked Jocelyn.

"Hmm," Perry hmmed. "You've turned up a mystery this time, Jim."

"But I know a little more about it now," Jim said. "Come and I'll show you what I found last night."

"Last night?" sqwerked Doris.

"Last night?" thought Brenda.

Jim took them to a slab that was four slabs away from the south-eastern corner. This slab looked the same as all the others around it.

"Last night," Jim said, "when the question of the floor kept rushing through my brain and keeping me awake,

I wandered out here. I don't know why I came to this corner … I was just walking and thinking and wondering. I was carrying a lit branch I'd taken from the campfire – it's more pleasant to walk in the night with a flame rather than a lantern, I've always found. Matter of fact, I once wrote a poem about this very thing, a short poem which—"

"Yes, yes," said Perry, who couldn't understand Jim's passion for poetry. "Get on with it."

"Well," Jim said, getting on with it, "I was standing just here when a small gust of wind came up, out of nowhere, really. It blew a little piece of burning wood off the top of my stick and onto the calico that covered this slab here.

"I bent down to smother the cinder, as I didn't want it to set fire to all the calico – that would have been a disaster. The floor underneath would have been charred black if all this fabric had gone up in a sea of blazing flame, intent on injuring the debris of more Time itself. Now *there's* an idea for a poem, don't you—?"

"Yes, yes," said Jocelyn. "What happened next?"

"Well, I managed to put out the flame, but not before it'd burned through a tiny bit of the calico. Look, see, just here, there're still a few bits of burned cloth. I held my lit branch above the hole, and… *Amehetnehet!*"

They all looked at him.

"You're a what-ne-what?" Doris asked.

"Amehetnehet," repeated Jim, more loudly.

"That's what I thought you said." She put her wing around his neck. "You're an archaeologist, Jim, and a poet, not a hetnehet."

"Amehetnehet. Amehetnehet, Amehetnehet, Amehetnehet!"

Perry looked worried. "Jim, how strong was the moon last night? Maybe it addled your brain a little."

"Dear, dear Jim," soothed Jocelyn Osgood.

Brenda moved her head close to the slab. "Quaaaoooo," she snorted in her down-here's-where-the-action-is tone.

Doris popped off Jim's shoulder and onto the slab. Perry and Jocelyn looked down also.

"Well I'll be worth two in the bush," Doris squawked. "Hieroglyphics!"

"So they are." Perry felt his moustache standing on end. "Decipher them for us, Doris, if you'd be so good."

"It's a cartouche," announced the macaw. "A royal cartouche. The name inside the border reads... 'Amehetnehet'."

"Amehetnehet," Jim repeated, still wondering why everyone had suddenly been so gentle and caring towards him a few moments ago.

"Amehetnehet?" Jocelyn scratched her curls. "I'm sorry, everyone, I don't have any idea what this means."

"Not surprising," Jim smiled. "Amehetnehet's hardly spoken of these days. Isn't that right, Perry?"

"Er, yes," Perry answered, trying to remember the last time he had heard anyone mention the word, and what the word referred to.

"In fact" – Jim rubbed his hands together – "until

last night, we'd never found any traces of anything to do with Amehetnehet."

"But what *was* Amehetnehet?" asked Jocelyn.

"You tell her, Perry."

Gerald Perry brushed his moustache this way and that as he tried to dredge up a memory of the word. "Well, y'see, long ago ... what I mean t'say is ... er, once there was ... in ancient ... er, Jim, I think you should tell everyone. You've got a much better way with words than me."

"Thank you, Perry, I'll send you my new collection of poetry if you feel that way. Well, Amehetnehet was one of the mightiest Pharaohs of the Fourth Dynasty in the Old Kingdom. He reigned about four and a half thousand years ago. We know that he was very popular and led the ancient Egyptian people to prosperity and long periods of happiness. The strange thing is, though, that there aren't many accounts left of Pharaoh Amehetnehet. We hardly know anything about him."

"No, that's right," added Gerald Perry in a voice that sounded knowledgeable.

"You see, no one's found any remains of any of his buildings, or any statues of him, or any stone tablets inscribed during his reign and listing his deeds. All we have is one papyrus scroll, found in 1906."

"Of course!" Perry's hands shot up into the air, as his memory re-ignited. "Now it's as clear as m'nose! Y'know who found that scroll, don't you, Jim?"

Jim smiled. "I remembered last night, when I found the cartouche. Bathsheba Snugg."

"Bathsheba Snugg!" crowed Doris.

"The woman who led us all here," Brenda thought.

"The woman who led us all here," Jocelyn said. "She certainly got around, didn't she?"

Perry nodded. "A scholar and a gentlewoman, was Bathsheba."

"This scroll she found," said Jim, "told of a colossal battle between the ancient Egyptians and the Nubians, far in the south. By a careful use of bronze mirrors, Amehetnehet's generals were able to reflect the sun directly into the eyes of their enemies. As the Nubians advanced on the Egyptian army, outnumbering the Egyptians by forty to one, the Egyptians flashed the light at them, harnessing the sun's brightness. The Nubians were momentarily blinded, and Amehetnehet's generals manoeuvred their chariots to encircle the enemy, and succeeded in capturing the entire Nubian army without a single drop of blood being spilled!"

"Extraordinary," Jocelyn gasped.

"Those were extraordinary times," said Cairo Jim. "According to the scroll Bathsheba found, Amehetnehet was thought to be the mastermind behind the whole mirror operation. This brilliant military feat was apparently typical of the cleverness and gentleness of this once great Pharaoh."

"I wonder what happened to him and his Dynasty," Perry mused.

"Now that," said Jim, "is a mystery about as big as this floor."

Perry looked down at the hieroglyphic cartouche again, and his heart tingled. "This is so fantastic," he beamed. "The only discovered thing, apart from the 1906 scroll, to do with Amehetnehet." He suddenly gave a small whoop of joy, locked his elbow through Jocelyn's, and, forgetting about his torn pants and the heat of the sun, twirled her around the slabs in a whirl of excitement.

"Mr Perry!" cried a startled Flight Attendant as she was whisked away across the limestone.

"Sometimes," Doris said to Jim and Brenda, "that man forgets how old he is."

"He's excited, my dear," said Jim.

"Quaooo," snorted Brenda, watching them twirling.

"Jim?"

"What, Doris?"

Perry continued to spin Jocelyn around the floor of stones.

"Do you think that all of this is what Herodotitis was writing about? The thing that was more marvellous than all of the Seven Wonders put together?"

"A monument so brilliantly constructed that it defies explanation?" added Jim, who had memorised what Bathsheba had written in her diary. "Hmm. Hardly seems likely, does it? It's just all flatness. Just a huge, empty floor. Nothing too remarkable about it, except for maybe its size."

Perry danced Jocelyn back to the trio, and came to a puffed halt. "Oh, but it *is* remarkable," he said, trying to catch his breath. "There may very well be clues somewhere else around here."

"Clues?" said Jim.

"Clues?" chirped Doris.

"Quaaooo?" snorted Brenda.

"Phew," puffed Jocelyn, wiping her moist forehead.

"Well," breathed Perry, "maybe."

"That gives me an idea," muttered Jim.

"I think you should keep sniffing round here, Jim, m'boy." Perry dabbed the back of his neck with his osnaburg handkerchief. "Meantime, all of this deserves the attention of the press!"

Jim whipped off his desert sun-spectacles, aghast. "Perry, I don't want to be in the papers again!"

"Oh, but y'must. You owe it to the world, Jim. If this is what Herodotitis was referring to, it should be splashed across every newspaper, blurted from every wireless, drawled from every television! Why, for goodness' sake, all that's left of one of the other Wonders, the Temple of Artemis at Ephesus, is a single column and lots of half-sunken marble slabs crawling with turtles! This beats *that* hands down!"

"But," began Jim.

"No buts about it. I've got mates on the *Egyptian Gazette* and on papers all over the planet. I'll get a press release out this afternoon, you see if I don't."

"I think it's a good idea, Jim." Jocelyn smiled. "You deserve a bit of recognition again."

But Jim didn't feel the same way about it as they both did.

△△△△△ 10 △△△△△

ENTER MR IMPLUVIUM

THAT EVENING, as the great limestone floor of Amehetnehet slowly cooled under the twilight-dusted calico, Mr Impluvium came forth into the world.

The breeze rippled his voluminous crimson-and-purple striped galabiyya as the clean-shaven man threaded his way between the sand dunes. Every few hundred metres he paused, took off his bowler hat, and wiped his sweaty forehead with the back of his hand. Then he put his hat back on and continued creeping towards the vastness.

Above him, like a greasy smear across the sky, Desdemona glided, keeping a blood-red lookout for Cairo Jim, Doris or the Wonder Camel.

Soon Mr Impluvium was coming close to the great ocean of calico. He stopped and stared at it, his caterpillar-like eyebrows creasing, a scowl of curiosity distorting his flabby lips.

"Arrrr," he murmured. He looked up, caught sight of the raven, and, with a wide gesture, signalled to her to come down.

With a silent swoop, she obeyed, and landed on his shoulder, being careful not to bump the brim of his bowler hat.

Impluvium put his manicured index finger to his lips. "Shhh," he whispered, his eyes narrowing into slits of secrecy. "Not a sound."

Desdemona winked at him, and quickly pecked a dozen fleas from her bellyfeathers.

Like an obese panther, the man tiptoed towards the edge of the calico. As he got nearer to it, Desdemona dug her claws into his shoulder.

"Careful," he hissed. "You're scratching!"

She gave a hoarse croak and relaxed her grip slightly.

Now they were at the very edge of the calico, and Impluvium was breathing heavily. With some effort, he crouched down – his pudgy kneecaps cracking loudly under the galabiyya – and grasped the fabric with his moist hands.

"Let us see what goody-goody-gumdrops has been spending a considerable portion of his existence in uncovering!" He slowly turned back the edge of the calico and rested heavily on his ball-like ankles. "Arrrr," he breathed, taking in the sight of the four slabs he had exposed.

"Craaaarrrrk," rasped his companion quietly.

For several minutes they said nothing as they looked at the limestone. Many thoughts filled the heads of man and bird: What was it part of? Why were the slabs so smooth and perfectly interlocked? How old were they? When could I gobble some more tinned Japanese seaweed? Why doesn't she bathe once in a while?

Then he spoke to her in a sideways snarl. "I bet you my last piastre that there're a whole lot more than these four slabs under all this material. Go on, hop it, Desdemona."

"Eh?"

"Hop under the calico and explore in there. Walk as far as the calico extends, and count the slabs for me." He held up the edge of the fabric.

"Me? Go in there?"

"Arrr."

"But I might suffer of cation under there!"

"Don't be ridiculous. It's only a light calico. Even a slug could breathe underneath it."

"But I'm not a slug!"

"That is a debatable point upon which whole volumes could be written, but we do not have the time for it now. Go on!" He grabbed her by her throat-feathers and shoved her under. Her claws squealed on the smooth limestone.

He watched as the shape of her moved (like a small, shrouded ghost) unsteadily to the left, then back to the right. Then her beak popped out from the edge and her eyeballs throbbed up at him.

"One question, Mr Impluvium."

"What? You're wasting precious seconds, you concealed creature of cretinitude!"

"What's the number that comes after three?"

He gave a huge sigh – he had completely forgotten that the bird could barely count. There would have to be another way for her to tally up the number of slabs. "Listen to me, Desdemona: don't bother to count them as you hop from one to the next. Instead, every time you land on a new slab, make some sort of noise. *I'll* do the counting, each time I hear your noise."

"Some sort of noise?" she asked.

"That's what I said, Little Miss Echo."

"Like this?" She let out a loud burp.

Impluvium shuddered. "If you must, yes."

She burped again. A pong of half-digested seaweed and stale bird-breath wafted into his face.

"Go on," he said, sitting heavily and pulling a cigar from his galabiyya pocket. "Get on with it!"

She burped once more and disappeared under the calico.

Impluvium lit his cigar with Bone's silver cigar lighter, and watched as the bulge of her body hopped, then burped, then hopped, then burped, then hopped and burped again. Every time she burped, he shuddered.

As his shudderings approached the hundred mark, he forgot about the cigar. By the time she had burped for the two hundredth time, the wad of tobacco had fallen from his fingers and burnt out on the sand next to him.

What, he wondered, *could this hugeness have possibly been part of?*

★   ★   ★

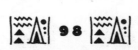

Outside his tent, Jim sat at his portable writing table, his face bathed in the glow from the kerosene lamp. Sheets of crumpled paper lay scattered across the table and around his ankles.

Doris, who had just finished her evening meal of snails and shergold cakes (sent up from Mrs Amun-Ra's in Gurna village), watched from her perch as he frowned over another sheet of paper. She thought she'd better give him some help, so she flew across and perched on the edge of the table.

"Rark," she rarked gently.

He looked up. "Hello, my dear."

"Salutations."

"I thought you and Brenda'd be playing cards at this hour."

"Not tonight," the macaw answered. "She's busy with Jocelyn Osgood, having her mane plaited or something. Brenda, not Jocelyn Osgood. I don't think Jocelyn Osgood has a mane. Yerk."

Jim smiled and looked over to the far side of the camp, where Jocelyn's hands were busy on Brenda's neck.

"I thought you might need some help."

Jim put down his pen and grimaced. "You know what I think we might have out there?" he asked.

"Tell me," Doris said.

"Well, seeing as how we haven't found any traces of building structures over Amehetnehet's floor, I'm starting to think that maybe a *floor* isn't what we've got at all."

Doris blinked in her tell-me-more way.

"No. We have to think differently. Perhaps we need to imagine so hard that our ribs hurt. Maybe that vast expanse of limestone is part of the *opposite* to a floor."

Doris blinked again. "A *roof*?"

"That's what I'm thinking. I got the idea this morning, when Perry said that there may be clues somewhere else round here. Now, there're no clues *above* the slabs, but there might be clues *below* them. Look."

He showed her the last piece of paper on which he'd been scribbling. At the top he had jotted the words *marvellous, astonishing, breathtakingly, ambitiously & stunningly built, defies explanation.* She looked carefully at his aerial drawing of the limestone slabs. Beneath it he had drawn a side view, slightly angled, and from each of the four corners he had drawn columns extending down to a horizontal line near the bottom of the page.

"Now see what happens if we do this," he said. He sketched more columns, all along the sides, all of them extending down to the line at the bottom.

"Rark. A temple," Doris said when he'd finished. "Amehetnehet's Temple."

"Perhaps," said Jim. "But it could be anything, any sort of structure that had a roof."

"Your brilliance outshines a thousand facets of the most luminous diamond," Doris squawked.

"Very good, Doris. Shakespeare?"

"No. Doris. I'm just saying how clever you are."

"I don't know about clever," he muttered, looking at

the drawing. "We just have to see things differently from how we're most likely to see them. To think of them in ways we wouldn't normally. Especially as we've so few clues to go on."

She hopped onto his forearm. "So, when do we start digging?"

"First light tomorrow. I think we'll begin at one of the corners. If there *are* any structures, like columns or anything, they might still be close to the floor."

"The *roof*."

"The roof. Thank you, my dear."

"You're very welcome," she cooed, and the feathers around her beak creased as if she were grinning.

The next morning Jim, Doris, Brenda and Jocelyn had barely started digging when Brenda's jaws grabbed Doris by the napefeathers and pulled her sharply backwards.

"SKKEEEEERRRRRRAAAAAARRRRKKKK!" screeched the bird as a heavy bundle of newspapers fell from the sky onto the sand where she'd been standing.

"What in the name of Ethel Merman!" shouted Jim, looking up. A small plane was flying off into the clouds.

Jocelyn grabbed the binoculars and watched it go. "A Lockheed Vega," she said. "There's something written on the side. 'EAT AT PERRY'S PIGEON RESTAURANTS FOR A MEAL YOU'LL NEVER...' I can't read the rest."

"It probably said 'digest'," muttered Doris.

"I'll have a word with him about his pilots," said Jim. "Doris, you could have been flattened. Are you okay?"

"Yep," she answered, shaking a little. "Thanks to Bren here." She hop-fluttered onto Brenda's snout and ran her wings all over Brenda's ears.

"Quaaaoooo," Brenda snorted – ear tickles drove her crazy in the most pleasant of ways.

Jocelyn untied the bundle. "Well, talk about fast!" She handed the top copy of the *Egyptian Gazette* to Jim.

The archaeologist-poet tilted back his pith helmet and scanned the front page through his desert sun-spectacles. There, amongst the stories of the day – a flood in Tanzania, a visit to Egypt by the Prime Minister of Zarundi, a fall in the price of dates and a story about a ship's purser who went mad at sea and who paraded about the decks thinking he was a donkey – was a bold headline:

CAIRO JIM MAKES HUGE DISCOVERY

Under this were ten paragraphs about the finding of the limestone slabs, and a photograph of Gerald Perry Esquire with the caption: *Cairo Jim's patron and friend, Gerald Perry Esquire (owner of Perry's Pigeon Restaurants), who was the first to announce the monumental find.*

"Hmm," said Doris, squinting at the photo. "Not a very recent pic, is it? He looks like he's barely old enough to exist."

"He always gives that photo to the press," Jim commented in a faraway manner. He was feeling decidedly uncomfortable about the coverage in the paper.

Brenda snorted as she read the story. "Quaaaooo!"

"The *Gazette*'s certainly excited about it," said Jocelyn, as she, too, read the article.

"Rark! It says here that it's probably the biggest and most enigmatic discovery of your career, Jim." Doris flexed her wings. "Enigmatic?"

"Mysterious," Jim answered absent-mindedly. "I wish Perry had waited a while. At least until we know a bit more..."

"Look, over by the camp!" Jocelyn was pointing to a distant cloud of sand rising near their tents.

"Quaooo!" snorted the Wonder Camel.

"Let's see," chirped Doris. She jumped from Brenda's forehead and grabbed the binoculars. "Well, they've swarmed, all right. Six television vans and some cars from the radio stations. I think you're wanted, Jim."

"Oh, dear," said Cairo Jim, wanting more than anything to be able to keep digging down into the sand.

"What's up with you?" rasped Desdemona as her companion read the newspaper. "If your lips were pursed any tighter I could put my small change in there. If I had any, that is."

Bone let out a bellyful of anger. "Arrrrrrrr! Take a look at this."

She hopped up onto the back of his chair and peered at the paper. "'GREAT FIND AT GIZA. MANY ANCIENT SLOBS IN SAND.' So what? There're plenty of slobs about, and I should know." She eyed him critically.

"That's *slabs*, not slobs, you illiterate inkblot of imbecility."

She squinted at the paper. "Hmph. You got a bit of ash from your stinky cigar on it."

"I'll get a bit of ash on *you* if you don't pipe down."

"Skrerk."

In a blur his hands scrunched the newspaper into a tight ball and hurled it onto the worn carpet. "This is no good, no good at all, Desdemona."

"No good, no good, no good," she echoed.

"First he finds all those stones out there, all of which are probably going to become the single most important find in the history of archaeology. Now he's got the media of the world all snivelling around him, falling at his feet and licking his soles."

"Yeccchhhhh," blurted the raven, her yellow tongue hanging out and her eyeballs throbbing as though she was about to be ill.

Bone stood and put on his bowler hat. "It is time," he announced, putting his pudgy hands on his hips, "for Mr Impluvium to take action."

△△△△△ 11 △△△△△

DIGGING DOWN

THE REST OF THE MORNING was a total write-off.

For nearly four hours, Cairo Jim was questioned and interviewed and interrogated by the newspaper journalists, the television reporters, the radio people and even by one man who wanted him to star in a Hollywood movie, playing himself and recreating the moment of discovery.

At first, Jim had straightened his spine and put up with it all, despite the fact that he was fairly shy. After a while, though, when the media kept on asking him what a 'hetnehet' was and why he thought he was one, Doris knew it was time to come to the rescue. She, Jocelyn and Brenda moved in and shielded their friend from the questions as best they could, helping him to answer them quickly and in a friendly manner.

(There was one very persistent young woman from a TV station in New York who insisted that she stay on with Jim at the dig and be with him every waking moment so she could be the first to break the story if he found anything further. Doris and Jocelyn saw how polite Jim was to her, but how the young New York woman was overwhelming him. For the first time, macaw and Flight Attendant worked

together, suggesting loudly that this woman should just fly on home again on the first available plane, lest she find a few desert scorpions lurking in her luggage. When last the New York woman was seen, she was being nudged by Brenda's snout, gently yet sturdily, back to her car.)

By this time Jim was almost hoarse from answering questions, and Brenda and Doris had shown all the reporters and others back to their vehicles. It was far too hot to continue digging down from the southern corner of the floor/roof.

"I don't know about you," Jim almost whispered to his friends, "but I'm going to rest for a while. Let's start work again at four this afternoon, yes?"

"Rark!"

"Good idea, Jim."

"Quaaaooo."

"Now listen to me carefully, for I am a busy man of huge importance, and detest having to repeat myself."

The old, leather-skinned stonemason nodded to the bossy stranger in the garish galabiyya and peculiar round hat. "Please, Mr Impluvium," the stonemason said, picking up a notepad and a stumpy pencil, "tell me what you want made, and I will chisel it quickly."

"How quick's quickly?" croaked the raven on the large man's shoulder.

"I need it as soon as is humanly possible," sneered Impluvium.

"Just tell me what it is you want me to make," said the man.

"A single slab of limestone, that is all." Thick, smelly cigar smoke poured from his mouth as he spoke.

"Only one?"

"Arrr. A single, simple slab that will change the course of History."

Late in the afternoon, when the heat of the day had passed, Jim and the gang returned to the stones and rolled the calico off the south-eastern corner. Then, carefully, he and Brenda prised up the corner slab (they had managed to loosen it before the bundle of newspapers had crashed down from the skies) and shifted it to the side.

"Right," puffed the archaeologist-poet, "let's go down."

He took his shovel and pierced the sand at the exact point where the corner slab had ended. With some effort, he pushed his foot down on the shovel, and the shovel sank into the hard, compacted sand.

Doris, Brenda and Jocelyn watched in silence.

"Mmm." Jim grimaced. He pulled the shovel up, and pitched the sand away. Three more times he dug at the points where he imagined a column should have ended. Three more times all he unearthed was hard, compacted sand.

He took off his pith helmet and scratched his head. "There's nothing here," he said. "Even by scraping

 107

the surface, I should've struck a column by now."

Doris flexed her wings and fluttered from Brenda's fore hump to the place where Jim had dug. "Maybe," she said, scratching in the sand with her claw, "there *is* a column here, but the top of it has crumbled. If we dig down a bit further, we might find the rest of it."

"She's right," said Jocelyn. "Maybe the top of the thing has eroded away."

"Quaaooo," Brenda snorted hopefully.

"Maybe the desert winds eroded it," squawked Doris. "Maybe the desert winds eroded the tops of *all* the columns. And the roof is being held in place by all the closely packed sand around it."

Jim thought for a moment. "I don't think it would've been eroded by the weather," he said. "This roof is pristine – there are no signs of weathering anywhere on it. The roof area would have eroded before the tops of any columns."

"Perhaps the columns were made from a softer stone than the limestone roof," Brenda thought with Wonder Camel insight. "They might have weathered away faster."

Jocelyn had a small shudder as the thought penetrated her curls. "Maybe the columns were made from a softer stone than the limestone roof," she said. "They might have weathered away faster."

"Rark. It's possible. That's why the roof hasn't been damaged. Dig a bit deeper, Jim. Let's find out."

Jim put his pith helmet back on and recommenced

digging. For twenty minutes he shovelled, down, down and further down. All he unearthed was more of the hard sand.

He put aside the shovel and squatted, inspecting the hole he'd made. "That's nearly two metres," he called up. "I think we'd have found some trace of anything by now."

Brenda had been snouting through the discarded sand, and pushing it this way and that with her hoofs. She had uncovered nothing except small rocks and ancient sand clods.

Doris waddled around the perimeter of the hole. "Here's a thought," she prerked. "Just suppose that the corners of the temple were more exposed than the sides. The winds and the whipping sands might've blasted the *four corners*, and the corner columns, more than the rest of the outside columns of the temple."

"We don't know for certain that this *was* a temple, my dear," Jim reminded her.

"For the sake of conjecturing, I'm calling it a temple," she squerked in a matter-of-fact, uniquely macaw tone. "Now listen: if it *were* the case that the outermost corner columns got more of the weather than the columns along the sides, then maybe the corner columns disappeared altogether. Worn down until there was nothing left. Over the course of Time."

Jim listened to her carefully.

"And if that's the case," she continued, blinking

109

excitedly, "then the columns on the sides would still be standing. It's possible."

"It is," said Jocelyn. "You are the brightest macaw I'm ever likely to meet, Doris."

Doris blushed beneath her feathers. "Oh, Jim taught me the art of Archaeological Conjecture," she muttered. "*He*'s the bright one."

"Rightio," Jim said, standing. "It's worth a try. And as it's your theory, my dear, why don't you pick a spot somewhere along the sides for us to look?"

He held out his arm and she fluttered up onto it. "Okay, then." She scanned the far edge of the roof, and started counting:

"B-R-E-N-D-A,
Ta Ra Ra Ra Boom De Ay,
fluff my feath-ers, go to town,
this is where we're digg-ing DOWN!

"The twenty-seventh slab from that end. Let's start there."

"Well, I can never argue with poetry," said Cairo Jim.

"What are they doing, fertiliser features?"

Desdemona had her eye glued to the telescope. "Digging," she croaked.

"Arrr. Whereabouts?"

"Somewhere. I dunno."

"Why don't you know?"

"I can't see 'em. All that sand they cleared when they uncovered the slabs is in my way."

Bone buffed his fingernails wearily. "Then how, you foolishly feathered numbskull, can you tell they're digging?"

"By all the sand that's flying up into the air, that's how. Sand doesn't fly up into the air by itself, you know. And it's not being blown; there's no wind about tonight. Sheesh, what d'you think I am? A moron or something?"

"Oh, heavens to the Goddess Betsy, how could I ever possibly think *that*?"

"It's still flying into the air," she rasped.

"Well, keep your eye on it. I want to know exactly when they've finished."

"Of course I'll keep my eye on it. There's not much choice, is there, since you super-glued my eyelid to the wretched telescope!"

"Arrrr."

12

SEEING THINGS DIFFERENTLY

"I DON'T KNOW WHY you contacted *me* about all of this," said the wiry, mole-like man as he followed Mr Impluvium and the raven across the darkened sea of calico.

"Because," Impluvium sneered, "as I explained on the telephonic instrument to you, this is a story of incredible newsworthiness. A scoop that will reveal a great fraud, a monumental shenanigan which has pulled the wool over the eyes of the world. Be careful with that candle, you stupid bird!"

"Ergh," Desdemona grunted, as the wax from the lit candle (strapped to the top of her skull) dribbled into her left eyeball.

"But why me?" asked the moleish man. "I am merely the gossip columnist and occasional Archaeological Tidbits reporter for the *Sudanese Camel Fanciers Weekly*. We are a very small magazine, Mr Effluvium."

"That's Impluvium." He clenched his cigar between his teeth impatiently.

"Why didn't you approach one of the bigger magazines or newspapers? The *Egyptian Gazette*, for example?"

"I favour the underdog, that's why. I think it will be

worthwhile for your magazine to break this story." *And, Bone thought smugly, it will be less suspicious for me if this is all revealed by a very small publication – it will add a smokescreen of quirkiness to what I have in store.*

"Why did we have to come here so early in the morning?" asked the man from the *Sudanese Camel Fanciers Weekly*. "By Hatshepsut's crown, it's not even daylight yet!"

"A great story such as this needs privacy for the time being."

"Here we are," croaked Desdemona, scratching at some fleas who were holding a convention below her bellyfeathers. "Show it to him, quick!"

"Roll back the calico, bird," Impluvium ordered.

With her grotty talons she obeyed.

"Wait a momentum," the reporter said as the stone slabs were revealed. "Isn't this the dig of Cairo Jim? The great stones of Amehetnehet?"

"Arrr."

"But all of this has already been reported in every paper and magazine I've seen. And on the wireless and television and in the newsreels at the cinema! You can't go anywhere without knowing about all this." He sucked his bottom lip in a mole-like way. "I'm sorry, Mr Deluvium—"

"Impluvium!"

"—but all of this has already been covered."

"Will you close that little mouth of yours and listen to me. Yes, Cairo Jim's finding of Amehetnehet's slabs *has* been covered by the press. Done to the After Life, if you ask me. The media flocked to it like flies to a gigantic honey pot. But what you are about to see now will be a revelation."

"A revelation?" repeated the reporter.

"One that will have those grubby newsflies swarming here once again. One that will prove that much of this discovery is one big hoax. A huge sham, designed to get that particular archaeologist maximum exposure in the worldwide press. A sort of contrived ego trip for Cairo Jim's own benefit, financially and – dare I say it – to satisfy his quiet lusting for glory!"

The reporter looked at him quizzically.

"Light up *our* find, my ludicrous lighthouse," Impluvium hissed at Desdemona.

"Yes, Mr Impluvium." She bent over, and the candle flame danced across the slab beneath her.

"Behold," purred the large man. "The piece that blows the whole discovery to smithereens!"

The reporter bent low and read the tiny inscription on the slab. Then he raised his head, looked at the gloating face of Mr Impluvium, and let out an astounded whistle into the early morning air.

At nine o'clock the next morning, Gerald Perry Esquire's Bentley ploughed across the sands to Jim's campsite. With a fierce spraying of sand, the car came to a halt, and Perry hurried out of the car and rushed to Jim.

"What in the name of Setiteti is happening, Jim? Heard a report on the radio this morning, right in the middle of the 'Yodelling Breakfast Hour'. Nearly choked on m'cornflakes, and got m'lederhosen all messed up badly. They said something about Amehetnehet's slabs being a hoax!"

Through his binoculars, Cairo Jim was watching the crowd of over a hundred media people clustering at the far edge of the calico. "We heard it too," was all he said.

"Rark!" Doris flapped her wings up and about. "It's misinformation!" she squawked.

"That it is," Jocelyn said worriedly as she saw the television cameras coming out.

Brenda, who was shifting back and forth nervously near Jim's tent, gave a low, uncertain snort.

Perry dabbed at his forehead with his handkerchief. "A hoax? I've never heard anything so preposterous, not since they invented edible shoelaces in case you got stuck in the desert with just a bottle of spaghetti sauce. Where would the press get information like this? How can it be a hoax?"

"They got it from a magazine," said Jim, taking the latest issue of the *Sudanese Camel Fanciers Weekly* from his back pocket and handing it to his patron. "We found this dumped outside when we woke. Page sixty-six."

"Whoever wrote it wears 'the very crown of false-hood'," Doris quoted from *Troilus and Cressida*.

Gerald Perry flicked to the page and read the article quickly. By the time he got to the end, his moustache was bristling, and his face had gone a bad shade of puce. "Who the devil is this Anton Scrivvel? How could he write such rot?"

"He's the gossip columnist and occasional Archaeological Tidbits reporter," said Jocelyn.

"It's not a hoax," Jim muttered, almost as though he had to convince himself that it wasn't. "We've got Bathsheba Snugg's research to back us up."

"What a hound!" Perry exclaimed.

"Quaaaoooo," Brenda snorted.

"Something's happening," Jim announced, still watching through the binoculars. "The crowd of media is parting a bit, and ... there's a man standing in the centre. A big, tall man, wearing a badly designed galabiyya and ... am I seeing correctly? A bowler hat on his head."

Doris winced her beak.

Jim refocussed the binoculars onto the figure. "He's raising his arms; I think he's about to speak. There go all the microphones, being pushed closer to him."

"I want to hear this," Perry growled. "Come on, let's go."

"No, Perry," Jim said softly. "I'm staying here."

"Eh? Oh, yes, m'boy, I understand. Stick to your ground. I won't be long."

With a terrible, cold hollowness starting to grip his insides, Jim watched Perry approach the throng.

"And," declaimed Mr Impluvium in a self-important voice, "that charlatan archaeologist has indeed hoodwinked each and every one of you. Not to mention the trusting people of the entire world, the people who held hope that here" – he waved his pudgy hand over the vast, flat calico covering – "was a part of a structure that might very well give us hope about something from the past. That might just lead us to some new knowledge, once possessed by our ancient ancestors, which has today been smothered by the cobwebs of modernity."

Gerald Perry was coming into earshot now, and he could hear what the big man was spouting.

"I have proof, ladies and gentlemen and everyone else, that what Cairo Jim has uncovered here is not the great, mysterious thing we have been led to believe it was. As you know, Jim has been claiming that all of these slabs represent some structure identified with the almost forgotten Pharaoh, Amehetnehet."

"Yes, yes," several reporters shouted.

"It is NOT! All of this has, I believe, nothing to do with Amehetnehet. It is a fraud, a huge, utter, fraud!"

"All of it?" asked a French journalist wearing glossy lipstick.

"That I am unsure of." Impluvium stroked his uppermost chin with his thumb and forefinger, in a well-rehearsed way. "Maybe *some* of this is old; perhaps a few of these stones are indeed from the ancient past. But I know for a fact that part of this huge expanse of stone slabs is *not* old. I have evidence that sections of this have been *recently* manufactured!"

A shocked gasp rose into the air, like stale air escaping slowly from a balloon.

"It is possible that Jim of Cairo may have stumbled across one or two genuine stone slabs around here. But that, I believe, is all he found. The rest is a mere contrivance."

This was all too much for Gerald Perry. "Go on, show us your proof, you big windbag!" he shouted.

"Oui, oui," yelled the French journalist. "Reveal your evidence."

"Yeah, show us!" the Americans called.

"Give us a squiz," some Australians said.

"Put your money where your mouth is," suggested someone with an accent that was hard to place.

"Roll out the barrel," yelled a man up the back. Everyone turned to stare, and he blushed deeply.

"I'll show you all with pleasure," smirked Impluvium. He moved to the left, squatted down, and grasped the calico in both hands. With a forceful wrenching, he ripped the calico clean asunder.

The noise of the cloth as it tore made Gerald Perry's skin crawl, and not only because he had paid for it.

Impluvium folded the torn material back neatly, until one single slab was revealed. "Gather around, ladies and gentlemen and everyone else. Here is the evidence!"

The crowd moved forward, some crouching, some kneeling, others standing, until the slab was surrounded on all four sides. Impluvium reached into his galabiyya and withdrew a long pointing-stick with a silver tip.

"This is what I discovered myself when I was taking my nightly walk the other evening. Look carefully."

He lowered the silver end of the stick to the slab, and ran it along one edge. "As you can all see, we have here undeniable proof of recent manufacture!"

The French journalist with the glossy lipstick had elbowed her way to the front of the crowd when they had all moved forward, and so she was closest to the area where Impluvium was pointing. Loudly she read the words that had been carved, in a neat and tiny copperplate style, into the stone:

"'Made by Sozan Stoneworks Company, 42 Neffer Square, Cairo. Ushabtis and Slabs For All Occasions. We Don't Carve By Halves!'"

The news people gave a huge, shocked gasp.

"As soon as I found this myself," Impluvium announced quickly, before the gasp had subsided, "I consulted the telephone directory. Sure enough, Sozan Stoneworks *does* exist at that location. The manager told me that a man wearing a jaunty pith helmet and special desert sun-spectacles, accompanied by a gold-and-blue-feathered macaw who was very talkative, and a mangy-looking Bactrian camel with exceedingly long eyelashes, had visited him, and ordered this slab to be made."

 119

"Lies," muttered Gerald Perry Esquire, but the crowd around him started to mutter other, harsher things about Cairo Jim, Doris and Brenda.

Impluvium had his audience right where he wanted them – in his fat, sweaty palm. He continued breathlessly: "I was naturally mortified when I made this discovery. To think that the well-known, dare I say *world-famous*, archaeologist Cairo Jim had actually contrived to HOODWINK each and every one of us. It filled me with a bristling sense of outrage!"

"Oui, oui," cried the French woman. "My outrageousness is bristling too! Right here! He tricked us all!"

"He took us for a ride, all right," agreed an American television reporter.

"Made us look like right galahs," seethed an Australian cameraman.

Perry could see that the crowd was becoming very restless: many people were talking to each other in tones of low, threatening harshness, and others were clenching and unclenching their fists and looking around furiously.

Impluvium surveyed the assembly, riding their anger as if it were a great wave on the ocean, and he were a world championship surfer. "I contacted an old friend of mine, Mr Anton Scrivvel of the *Sudanese Camel Fanciers Weekly*. It was Anton who broke the story, and that, in a nutshell, is why we are all here."

The press started to growl.

"I'm sorry, ladies and gentlemen and everyone else," said Mr Impluvium, holding up his hands apologetically. "But Cairo Jim has tricked you all. This is not a monument to the Pharaoh Amehetnehet. I believe it is nothing more than a boring, antediluvian dance platform, if that. This so-called discovery is about as important as a fingernail!"

"We'll wipe the world with Cairo Jim!" shouted a bristling reporter from a cable television network. "Wait till we break the story!"

"We'll break *him*!" someone yelled.

The crowd agreed noisily.

Being a man of great experience, Perry knew there was no sense in trying to argue with mounting anger of this scale. He quickly decided that it would be better to hurry back to Jim and his friends and get them away from here, before the crowd turned really nasty.

Off he rushed across the calico.

"Friends," Impluvium said, "please do nothing hasty. Just because this – I must say it – *charlatan* archaeologist and his cohorts have duped all of you into believing what he has claimed; just because he has made total donkeys' posteriors out of each and every one of you; just because he has nearly ruined all your professional reputations and the reputations of your newspapers and magazines and television networks and radio empires and whatnot; just because he has abused the trust and goodwill of the ENTIRE WORLD which waited breathless for more news of this discovery, why, that is no reason to take violent measures against the fraudulent Jim of Cairo, whose campsite happens to be" – Impluvium paused long enough to let a wide, contemptuous smile spread across his face – "over THERE!"

He flung his striped arm in the direction of Jim's campsite, pointing with the silver end of his stick, and all the heads turned sharply.

"Let's get some footage of the slimeball," shouted a burly photographer.

"Let's rip down that tent of his!" screamed another, his voice almost strangled by his anger.

"Rip it to pieces!"

"Let's teach him a lesson he'll NEVER forget," cried the French woman. "Come on, Media of the World!"

A deep roar went up, from every throat of every man, woman and everyone else present. Across the calico they swarmed, like a plague of uncontrollable locusts intent on absolute destruction.

"Hurry," Perry urged, as Jim and Jocelyn tried to bundle Brenda into the back of the Bentley. "It's as I thought – that man has turned them completely!"

"*Quaaaooooo!*" snorted Brenda, terrified as she heard the shouting and yelling coming closer. The back seat area was too small, and she was struggling to fit.

Doris darted to her prized Shakespeare first edition and started dragging it to the car.

"Jim, this is terrible!" yelled Jocelyn. "They're out for blood!"

Dozens of microphones and small tape-recorders were being hurled through the air at them, one of them narrowly missing Doris.

"*SKREEEEEERRRRRRRRRKKKK!*"

"Come on!" Perry shouted, revving the engine wildly. "Let's get to the Old Relics Society! It's safe there!"

"In you go, Bren!" Doris shoved her Shakespeare into Brenda's lap, and then started to push the Wonder Camel's rear hump into the car.

"*QUUUAAAAAAOOOOOOO!*"

"Quickly!" Perry shrieked.

Brenda grunted shrilly. A Dictaphone whizzed past her ears.

The crowd was almost upon them when Brenda managed to exhale fully, and her humps deflated just enough for her to slide down onto the back seat. Jim helped Jocelyn swiftly into the front passenger seat next to Perry, and, taking one last look at his campsite and the rush of hostility that was about to engulf it, the archaeologist-poet leapt onto the running board with his knapsack over one shoulder and Doris perched tightly on the other, and the car went tearing off over the sandhills.

13

INVERSION!

"BUT IT'S NOT A HOAX," said Cairo Jim in the smallest of voices.

He, Doris, Brenda and Jocelyn had been listening to the evening radio news in the Sanctuary Room of the Old Relics Society. They had learned that the marauding media had earlier that day destroyed the campsite, ripping apart the tents and smashing Jim's table and chair and Doris's perch and all their other belongings.

"Never mind, my lovely," Jim said to Brenda, who was sitting silently in the corner. "I'll buy you all the Melodious Tex western novels you want when all of this blows over."

"Quaaoo," she snorted sadly.

Jocelyn sat next to the Wonder Camel, wondering if the crowd had vandalised the montgolfier Persephone. There had not been time to go back to find out, as Jocelyn had to fly out with Valkyrian Airways in less than two hours' time for a three-week trip to the Ivory Coast and the Belgian Congo. She had phoned the balloon's owners and advised them of its location. She wanted to spend her last few valuable hours in Cairo here with her friends.

"Rark," Doris rarked. For once, there was not much more she could say.

"What really upsets me," Jim said, "is we can't go back. I really thought we might be onto something there, digging down from the edges of the slabs. Even though we hadn't yet uncovered anything under them, there was the *possibility*. Now what do we do?"

"Let me answer that one for you." Perry bustled into the Sanctuary Room, his eyes filled with dismay but also with a small bit of hope.

"Have you heard the news?" Doris asked him. "It's on all the radio stations, everywhere. We even picked up the short-wave frequency to Outer Mongolia. They're calling Jim a fraudster!"

"Hmm." Perry sat and rubbed his moustache. "Forget about all of that, Jim. *You* know this isn't a hoax, and *I* know it isn't. Let all of this die away."

"But my reputation," Jim said.

"Your reputation is more solid than this sandstorm in a teacup," said Perry.

Jim looked doubtful as he fiddled with his pith helmet in his lap.

"Now listen, I'm sending you back to work."

"Rerark! We can't go back there! We'll get attacked by all those press people!" Doris was spluttering, her beady eyes blinking rapidly. "And we heard on the news that the public are waiting for us, with big sticks and—"

"No, no, no," Perry hushed her, "not to work at the stones of Amehetnehet. Goodness gracious, Doris, I

 125

may be getting on, but I'm not daft. No, I firmly believe that in a situation like this, the best thing to take your minds off all the nastiness is good, solid work. Especially for an archaeologist. It's the best remedy, you'll find."

Jim sighed. He didn't seem very enthusiastic.

"What are you suggesting?" Jocelyn asked.

"Well," said the elderly man, "for some months now the Society here has been thinking of mounting a small-scale dig inside the Great Sphinx at Giza. There's some preservation work to be carried out on the interior walls; some rising damp from the water table under the sand is getting into the Sphinx's foundations. She needs to be damp-proofed from within."

Jim stopped fiddling with his pith helmet.

"We weren't going to give it to you, Jim – it's only a small sort of project, and you're more important than that – but now, in light of what's just happened, it seems you and Doris and Brenda are just the team for the job. It'll keep you out of the public eye – you'll actually be camping deep inside the Sphinx – and maybe it'll keep your mind off this nastiness."

"Plus," Doris squawked, "we won't be far away from the stones of Amehetnehet! Maybe we can get back to them, when all those people with sticks have gone away."

"No," said Perry, a tiny twinkle in his eyes. "I wouldn't advise you to go near Amehetnehet's stones, not for a long while. We've roped off the area from the tourists and those who wish to write rude graffiti about all of you on the slabs. When this business blows over, we'll see about resuming work on the Amehetnehet dig."

"Into the Sphinx, eh?" Jocelyn smiled at Jim. "What do you think of that, my friend?"

"I suppose it's something," he said flatly. "And something is what we really need right now."

"And when I had them *really* roused, it was the most incredible feeling, Desdemona! Like controlling electrical current, surging it through my very fingertips! Arrrrr!"

"You did well, my Captain," she croaked.

"And better is yet to come," he purred sneeringly as he watched the evening settle through the cracked window of the Whiff of Nefertiti Perfume Parlour.

"There's one thing I don't get."

"What's that, you dimwitted dustcatcher?"

"Well, why did you tell all them journos that some of those slabs *might* be genuine and ancient? Why not just say that the whole lot was a hoax? That Jim had manufactured all of it?"

"Because I am a genius, that's why." He manicured his forefingernail delicately.

"Eh?"

"If I had told them that all of the slabs were fakes, I would have shut the door on myself. By creating the possibility that some of those slabs are genuine – which of course they *all* are, except for *my* bit of handiwork – I am able to get on with my Plan of Return."

Her eyes throbbed at him in a tell-me-tell-me-tell-me way.

"I am going to capitalise on it, Desdemona. I am going to go out tomorrow and start my return into the world." He lowered his voice, and his eyebrows bristled with the greatest excitement he had known in a very long time. "The slabs of Amehetnehet are going to help me rebuild my reputation. But more importantly, they will help the world to see me as I truly am. Mr Impluvium here is not permanent; he is merely a stage in the rebirth of Neptune Flannelbottom Bone."

"The *rebirth*?"

"Yes, you feathered slimeball, the rebirth."

"Huh?"

"I am coming BACK!"

"Back? You mean...?"

"From the very depths of the dead, Desdemona. From the After Life I will return. And finally, at last, the world will give me the glory I so richly deserve, and which has been so long overdue!"

She was croakless at his brazenness.

In the candle's flame his eyes danced with horrible delight. "And what's more, I will have managed to completely invert *my* reputation with that of Cairo Jim! HOW SWEET IT SHALL BE! *Aaaaaarrrrrrrrrrrrrrrrrrrr!*"

Part Three:

INTO THE SPHINX

NOWNESS OF THE TIMES

AT FIRST, DORIS – who had a natural, birdlike fear of small enclosed spaces – had dreaded the idea of being inside the Sphinx. But when they arrived under cover of the night, and after Perry had opened the small, secret door in the Sphinx's hindquarters and had helped her and Jim and Brenda inside with all their supplies, the macaw began to change her mind.

The great statue's interior was roomy, and not at all cramped. At its highest point the ceiling was more than nine times as high as Cairo Jim, and tapered gradually down towards the sides and the front, where the Sphinx's paws extended outside. In these paw and side areas, Jim could still stand upright, with no danger of banging his pith helmet against the limestone above him.

Only the body-chamber of the Sphinx was hollow; the head section and most of the front paws were walled off from the body, forming separate sections.

Perry had obtained for them a new camp table, chair, stretcher, mattress and pillow, spirit stove and kerosene lanterns, twelve dozen tins of food (he promised to deliver fresh food every third night), cooking utensils, a spare perch and Shakespeare stand for Doris, a comfy Persian rug and some old Melodious Tex western

adventure novels for Brenda, a few plump and faded cushions from the Old Relics Society, and thirty large bottles of purified water.

After Perry had left them, Jim and Brenda started stacking the food and water against the wall where the Sphinx's right paw extended.

"Hmm," muttered Doris, who was flitting around near the top of the chamber – the underneath of the Sphinx's back. She flew slowly along the length of the limestone, along the inside of the statue's spine. "Guess what?"

Jim, who was arranging the food, separating the tinned vegetables from the tinned fruits, looked up sadly at her.

Brenda, who was making the stack of water bottles neater, snorted. "Quaooo?"

"What is it, my dear?" Jim asked.

"There're small shafts up here – ten of 'em. No wider than pencils. They go up at an angle." She hovered by one of the shafts and squinted through it. "Yep, all the way up to the outside."

"Air channels," Jim said.

"Time channels," Doris squawked, still squinting into the shaft. "It's eighteen minutes to eleven."

Jim still didn't know how she did this, but under the circumstances his curiosity was dampened, and he didn't ask her.

"At least, with those channels," Brenda thought, "we'll be able to breathe easily."

"At least with those channels," said Jim, stacking another tin, "we'll be able to breathe easily. Which is more than we could do out there, I guess."

Brenda came over to him and nuzzled him gently in the back of his shirt. He almost smiled.

Doris flew down to land on the tins of desserts – Malawian snails for her and imported Mabutoland worms for Brenda (Perry had spared no expense to obtain the best) – which Jim hadn't stacked yet. "Rark! Don't fret, Jim, we'll be okay." She opened her beautiful wings and winked at him. "We always have been okay in the past, haven't we?"

He sighed – a heavy, brick-like sigh that seemed to shudder all the way up his throat. "Things have never been as bad as this," was all he said before he started stacking the tins again, slowly and without enthusiasm.

Every night, around midnight, when nobody was about, the trio would creep out the small door in the Sphinx's hindquarters and walk and fly across the sand dunes for half an hour, to stretch their legs and wings and to get great lungfuls of the cool, desert air.

Sometimes they would collect the fresh food, daily newspapers and other supplies Perry left for them in a small pit, under a large rock, at an arranged sand dune.

On these walks, Cairo Jim couldn't bring himself to go anywhere near the roped-off limestone slabs of Pharaoh Amehetnehet. It was as though he was paralysed by the past.

★ ★ ★

During their fifth night inside the Sphinx, while Jim was sitting at the table and trying to write a brief report to Perry, Doris hopped up onto the arm of his camp chair. She had just been reading the previous day's copy of the *Egyptian Gazette*.

"You know," she squawked, "the press are still on about us. They say we're scoundrels and we've gone to ground. Hiding from the public. Rark!" Her feathers bristled indignantly. "How can they write such rubbish, Jim?"

The archaeologist-poet laid down his pencil and looked at her. He took a deep breath and tried – very hard, and for the first time since the nastiness had occurred – to sound positive, and like his normal self. "They write that because of the *nowness* of things."

She blinked at him. "The nowness?"

Brenda, sitting quietly in the corner, listened carefully.

"The heat of the moment," he explained. "Right now, it's easy for the press to whip up the popular opinion out there, without caring about the true facts." He took a big breath, and straightened his spine. "But don't worry, my friends. The one thing that we always work to uncover will sort this out."

"Eh?" said Doris.

"Quaaoo?" snorted Brenda.

"*History*. History, which we're constantly looking for, will reveal who the villains were. And who was innocent."

Doris moved closer to him then, and rubbed her head up and down against his arm. "Good to have you back," she warbled. "Good to have you back."

Later that night, after their walk outside, Brenda was the first to notice that Jim wasn't *quite* back.

The Wonder Camel was sitting against the rear wall inside the Sphinx, a little distance from the table where Jim was sitting. She saw the tiny drops of clear liquid glistening by the lamplight.

She gave a tiny snort to Doris – a snort that Doris knew meant for her to observe. The caring, noble macaw looked up, first at Brenda, then at their human companion.

Silently, as the lamplight flickered high against the inside walls of the Great Sphinx, they watched the tears coursing slowly down Cairo Jim's cheeks and plopping onto the blank sheet of writing paper in front of him.

△△△△△ 15 △△△△△
CARVING A PLACE IN HISTORY

"CRARK! Why is it that every time we have to go out at night, you have to strap one of these infernal candles to the top of my skull?"

Mr Impluvium sneered at his whingeing companion as she hop-fluttered across the sand. "Do you think," he sneered, his lips curling around his stinking Belch of Brouhaha cigar, "that *I* would carry such a thing? My fingers are far too important to risk having hot wax spilt on them. Heaven forbid!"

"And I suppose my headfeathers ain't important?"

"Let me put it this way: on the Global, Universal Scale of Recognised Importance, your head rates slightly lower than a half-dead slug."

Desdemona thought about this for a second, then said, "Thank you very much."

"You are most welcome. Arrr, look, we're here."

His pudgy hands lifted the barrier rope at the stones of Amehetnehet, and with a grunt he bent down and ducked beneath it. "This wretched galabiyya," he hissed, hitching the garment from one of the many sweaty crevices of his huge body. "The sooner I can bring back my esteemed self into the world, and don my plus-fours trousers and spats again, the better."

 135

"Yergh," shuddered the raven. She had never cared for his taste in fashion.

"Quickly, Desdemona, time is not a commodity of which we are blessed with an over-abundance at the moment. It is imperative that we act swiftly over the next few days, if my Great and Breathtaking Plan of Total Re-evaluation of the Entire History of the World is to take place."

She scuttled across the slabs after him, trying to keep the candle's flame steady, and thinking that if ever that montgolfier they had seen earlier got a leak and needed to be inflated again, she knew *exactly* where to find all the hot air.

Presently he came to where he wanted to be: the precise centre of the great expanse. He squatted down heavily. "All right, you nocturnal node of nastiness, rip this calico further, about two square metres from here to here, and tear it to shreds. Tear it to Kingdom Come. And be quick about it!"

"Aye, aye, my Captain." The sooner this was all done, and the sooner they were back at the perfume parlour, the sooner she could get rid of the stupid melting candle.

"Mr Impluvium! Remember, as long as I am dressed like this, I am Mr Impluvium!"

"Yes, Mr Impluvium." She lowered her razor-sharp beak and, in a frenzied flash of savage seconds, ripped the calico to pieces.

"Arrr, now sit still and watch. And try not to distract

me with your inane babblings. What I have to do is vitally important."

She pecked at a few fleas under a wing (the flame bobbed and almost went out) and then lay down on her belly, propping her head and beak in her wingtips as she watched him. "Okay, big boy, entertain me."

"Shut your beak, before I shut it with something you will not welcome!"

"Okay, okay, don't get your galabiyya in a knot."

"Now, don't bat an eyelid."

"Don't talk to *me* about eyelids. One of mine is still glued to that telescope back at the perfume parlour."

"Shhhh!"

He leant forward until he was kneeling, and slid his hand up and under the galabiyya. Desdemona watched his hand scrabbling about under the fabric like a mole digging a confused tunnel under the ground. He took out a hammer and chisel.

His lips curled into a grin of vandalistic glee, and he puffed heavily on the cigar. He positioned the chisel on the slab in front of him – a genuine slab, not the one he had had made – and gave a sharp tap with the hammer.

CLINK! A small but damaging sound rose into the night.

"Here's another little jewel in my crown," he muttered, his hands going to work with great delicacy as he chiselled into the ancient limestone. "And another hefty nail in the sarcophagus of Cairo Jim."

CLINK!

"Arrrr."

CLINK!

"Arrrrrr."

CLINK! CLINK!

"Arrrrrrrr. Arrrrrrrrrr. Arrrrrrrrrrrrr!"

Early the next day, Mr Impluvium and his raven paid another visit to the Sozan Stoneworks Company.

"Here," he commanded, thrusting a large, grubby drawing onto the stonemason's workbench. "Do you think you can manage this?"

"Another slab?" asked the stonemason.

"Examine the drawing," smirked Impluvium. "You will see there is much more this time."

The old eyes of the stonemason narrowed, the grit-filled creases around them – creases filled with a lifetime of hewing stone and carving rocks and working with the mighty earth – crinkling deeply as he surveyed the shapes and structures that Bone had drawn after his chiselling expedition.

"Yes," he said at last. "There is much work here, but I am able to complete it with the help of my sons."

"I am pleased to hear it," said the fleshy man in the bowler hat. "I will need all of those structures delivered in the night time, one week from tomorrow."

"But, Mr Impluvium, you still haven't paid me for the slab I made for you."

"Payment?" The hairiness above Impluvium's eyes

bristled indignantly. "Arrr. Have no fear, my good man, I shall pay you *fourfold* when you have completed this work."

"But—"

"All right, *five*fold. But not a piastre more, you understand." He lowered his voice and leant menacingly close to the old stonemason. "You might even consider doing this job for the glory of the world to come, if you get my meaning..."

The old man stepped back from the prune-like stench of him.

"Good man," Impluvium said, in a patting-on-the-head type of voice. "I will telephone you in two days to see how things are progressing. Come, bird!"

Before the stonemason could utter another word, Impluvium turned on his heel and left the premises, his galabiyya billowing as he strode off.

"Crark! You told him!"

He held out his hand. "Taxi!" he shrieked at a passing cab.

"Where're we going now?"

"To the newspaper offices. We have a rendezvous with the press."

"Rhonda *who*?"

"Shut up, slughead."

△△△△△ 16 △△△△△

PERRY BRINGS NEWS

JIM WAS TAKING A MOISTURE SAMPLE of the Sphinx's interior left haunch when the small door in the Sphinx's hindquarters swished open and Gerald Perry Esquire hurried in, hunched and worried-looking.

"Jim, Doris, Brenda! There's something going on at Amehetnehet's stones!"

Cairo Jim put down his small Dampness No More! Archaeological Swabbing Cloth. "What? What's happening?"

Perry plonked himself into the camp chair and caught his breath. "I heard it this morning, at the Old Relics Society. Got it off our special news service. He's obviously gone to every media outlet he could!"

"Who has?" screeched Doris, flexing up and down on her perch.

"That Impluvium man. The one who turned everybody against us." Perry took off his desert sun-spectacles and puffed loudly.

Jim felt a small glow of solidarity warming his chest when he heard Perry say *us*.

Brenda gave a tell-us-more snort and rolled her head in a circle.

"He's called a press conference," Perry said gravely.

"There're hundreds of journos out there, people from the television and wireless and the glossy magazines. Every man, woman and his or her dog has turned up!"

"Dogs?" Doris blinked. "What would dogs be doing there? Since when do they—?"

"Figure of speech," Jim told her.

"Rerk. *Another* one." *Humans have a funny way with words,* she thought. *Apart from Mr Shakespeare, of course.*

"What's he telling them?" Jim asked.

"He hasn't started yet." Perry looked at his watch. "He announced the press conference to start in fifteen minutes. I'm going to go and skulk at the outer extremities of the crowd. Hear what the swine has to say. Then I'll come back and fill you three in."

"Rark, won't you be recognised? The papers have just started dragging your name into this as well."

"Doris is right," Jim agreed. "Some of those reporters are bound to know you."

"Thought of that." Perry reached into his blazer pocket and pulled out a pair of spectacles with a false rubber nose, crepe-hair moustache and bushy eyebrows attached. He slipped the disguise onto his face. "There. No one'll know me *now*."

"SKRRREEEEEERRRRRRRKKKKKKK!" skrree-eeeerrrrrkkkkkked Doris, who got a sudden fright when she looked at him.

Perry jumped in the chair but quickly regained his composure.

Brenda gave an admiring snort.

"Glad you like it, Brenda," Perry said, standing and making for the door. "Now don't worry, I'll be back here as soon as I've heard what he's up to."

"Be careful," Jim said.

Perry winked behind the strange spectacles and artificial nose and hairy bits. "Careful is my middle name," he said, before ducking outside.

"I always thought it was Marion," Jim said.

"Behold!" cried Mr Impluvium to the enormous throng of reporters and journalists assembled by the perimeter rope at the slabs of Amehetnehet. "I show you a discovery of great startlingness!"

Gerald Perry slid unnoticed into the back of the crowd and stood on tiptoes to watch the bowler-hatted man who was sweating a lot in the blaze of the sun.

"The Trustees of the Old Relics Society have granted me permission to continue the excavations here at the stones of Amehetnehet," Impluvium boomed in a rich, self-important voice.

A dozen or so reporters gave a small clap at this news.

"*Liar!*" thought Perry angrily. "*Fibber, dirty rotten distorter of the truth!*" But he didn't say anything, for fear of being attacked by the mob.

"I am grateful to the Society for such a chance," Impluvium continued, "and I have asked you all to gather here today, ladies and gentlemen and everyone else, to witness the latest of my discoveries at this mysterious site."

He pulled out his pointing-stick with the silver tip. "Here is what has startled me so!"

He held the stick above his head, so that it pointed straight up at the sky. All of the eyes in front of him looked skywards, then to the silver end of the stick. With a great, bold, sweeping gesture, Impluvium sliced through the air in a wide arc. Every set of eyeballs before him followed the arc, staying glued to the silver end of the stick, until it came to rest on a single slab in front of Impluvium's fat and sweaty sandals.

Small murmurs of curiosity came from the front of the crowd.

Impluvium took a deep breath. "A cartouche," he announced with a flourish of his eyebrows. "A genuinely ancient cartouche, unlike the *modern* rubbish that Cairo Jim laid here to trick us all."

"Cad," muttered a man in the middle of the crowd at the sound of Jim's name.

"I have dated this slab of limestone, and I can tell you, as a representative of the Old Relics Society, that the stone was laid 4,897 years, 243 days, 16 hours and" – he looked at a miniature sundial strapped to his wrist – "forty-one minutes ago. Give or take a few seconds."

The reporters were impressed, many of them scribbling into their notebooks or muttering into their small tape-recorders.

"But the most exciting thing," smiled the fleshy man, running his stick around the cartouche, "is the name inside this cartouche. For those of you who do not understand hieroglyphics fluently, allow me to read this for you."

He paused, struck a learned stance, and looked down at the cartouche.

"'Bonelaten'," he read, pronouncing the O like the O in the word *god*.

"Bonelaten?" went the name through the crowd.

"*Bonelaten?*" thought Gerald Perry.

"The great God-King Bonelaten," Impluvium said. "Ladies and gentlemen and everyone else, what you are standing by is *not* the remains of a structure belonging to the obscure and forgotten Pharaoh Amehetnehet. That was all part of Cairo Jim's Grand Concoction, to achieve fame and self-glory. No, my friends, what we have here" – and his pointing-stick swept across the huge expanse of slabs – "are the remains of the Grand Resurrection Temple of Pharaoh Bonelaten!"

There was a mad flurry of scribbling, and a steady hum of urgent mutterings into tape-recorders. Many flashbulbs popped brightly in Impluvium's smug face.

Perry felt his spine bristling with outrage and anger.

"And," Impluvium went on, "in a few short days, I will be issuing another invitation to you all to return here and behold the next stage in this monumental discovery."

"The next stage?" a woman asked.

"Arrr," he nodded. "With the backing of the Old Relics Society, I, Mr Impluvium, will be personally responsible for a total and authentic reconstruction of the Grand Resurrection Temple of Bonelaten!"

The scribbling and muttering were earnest now.

"Yes, good people of the world's press, very soon you shall see what this Temple would have *originally* looked like. Thanks to my careful and assiduous research into similar ancient temples of the period, you will be astounded at the architectural detail with which I'll have recreated this building, and you shall be able to partake in a tasty afternoon tea at a small kiosk I will be adding."

"Scones?" asked a hefty cameraman, taking his eye from his camera and looking very interested.

"Scones, meringues, lamingtons!" answered Impluvium. He gave a wide grin. "Even ... petits fours!"

"Ooh la la," said the French reporters present.

At that point, Gerald Perry Esquire slipped quietly away and headed back to the Sphinx.

"The Grand Resurrection Temple of *whom*?" asked Cairo Jim, his eyes wide.

"Pharaoh Bonelaten," answered Gerald Perry, plonking himself into the camp chair and taking off his false nose, spectacles and eyebrows.

"Rark!" Doris jerked up and down on her perch. "Never heard of him!"

"Nor I," Jim said, frowning.

Brenda snorted loudly – the name was a mystery to her as well.

"Y'know what I think, Jim?" Perry threw his disguise onto the floor and clenched his fists in his lap. "I think that this Impluvium character is a big fat fake. I reckon he's making the whole thing up! Pharaoh Bonelaten indeed. Why, if there ever was a Pharaoh named Bonelaten, I'll show you a cat that can play the piano!"

"But why?" Jim scratched his head. "What's Impluvium got to gain from all of this?"

"Rerark, and who *is* Impluvium? Where'd he crawl from?"

Perry stood. "Y'know what I'm going to do?"

"What?"

"Rerk, what?"

"Quaoo, quaoo?"

"I'm going to go back to the Old Relics Society right now and call a press conference of my own! We'll soon reveal Impluvium to be the charlatan he really is!" He put on his hat and made for the hindquarter door.

Jim held out his arm. "No, Perry."

"Eh?

"No," said the archaeologist-poet quietly. "Not yet. Let's give him the chance to show what he's really up to. I have a feeling that with a little more time, Impluvium – whoever he is – will unravel more rope to hang himself with."

BATHSHEBA SNUGG'S CLUE

TWO DAYS LATER, UNDER THE COVER of the calm night, the person known formerly to the world as Captain Neptune Flannelbottom Bone steered a massive truck across the rough road leading to Giza.

"Look out there, Desdemona," he purred. "All those Amehetnehet stones. Just waiting for a Recycler of History, such as what I am, to come along and use them to make my world a better place! Arrrr!"

Sitting on the dashboard, Desdemona squinted at him and scowled her beak – ever since he had shaved off his beard and adopted the appearance of Mr Impluvium, she couldn't help thinking how much he looked like an overfed piglet on a pair of stilts.

"*That*," he went on, "is the best thing about History: a genius can take it and turn it to his advantage."

"I wanna know something," she rasped, her eyes throbbing.

"What do you want to know, you ornithological orifice?"

"What're you gonna do with all that stuff in the back of the truck? All them enormous columns and arches and miniature sphinxes and those fifty statues of that ugly Pharaoh?"

Impluvium glared at her. "He is *not* ugly, you cretin. I had Mr Sozan sculpt those statues of the Pharaoh Bonelaten from a photographic likeness of myself."

"They look like fifty fatballs in bad skirts," she said. "And they all look like they've just stepped in something yucky!"

Impluvium swiped at her and she hopped quickly to the far side of the cabin.

"You are beneath my contempt. All of that in the back of the truck is going to become part of the reconstruction I told the press about."

"Huh?"

"We are going to *erect* all of those pieces, on top of Amehetnehet's stones. We shall build a temple the likes of which the ancient world has never, EVER seen, one that will be so grand, so vast, so fantastically designed, that it will bring waterfalls of tears to the eyes of everyone who beholds it! Compared to what *we* will construct, the Hanging Gardens of Babylon will seem like a wonky garden shed."

"*We?*" she asked, in a voice that sounded as if she'd just eaten something that had been dead for far too long.

"Arrr. We."

"*You and me* are gonna put all those huge things up?"

"That's right, bilious breath."

"Oh, pickle me rancid! How can just the *three* of us put all of that up?" (Arithmetic was, of course, a mystery to the raven.) "It'll take us as long as it took to build the pyramids! Why don't we get some strong, burly men or women to help us? I know for a fact that the Turkish Women's Championship Tent Erection Team ain't busy at the moment."

Impluvium steered the truck carefully off the road, and onwards through the sand dunes. "You forget my genius, Desdemona. You see, I know from bitter experience that the more people I involve in one of my Utterly Great and Brilliant Plans, the more chance there is for the Plan to go wrong. Hence I made sure that Sozan constructed all of these pieces of stonework from the *lightest* and at the same time the *strongest and most durable* stones available."

"Eh?"

"Yes, yes, yes. Spiffystone."

"Spiffystone?"

"Arrr. The latest in decorative durability. Every bit of sculpture back there – every column and arch and lintel and pedestal, each stairway and ziggurat and all those fifty statues of that handsome Pharaoh – is so light that I myself, without the aid of anyone else, can pick it up and move it to where I want it. It is merely a matter of super-gluing the pieces into place."

"And it'll all last?"

"Oh, yes, yes, yes indeed. Spiffystone will last as long as you want. It won't erode. No desert winds, no sandstorms, no graffiti-minded tourists or rude birds intent on staining things will be able to destroy these!"

The headlights bobbed across the mounds of sand and rocks ahead. Desdemona gobbled a flea from her tailfeathers and tried to let all this information sink into her skull.

"No," Impluvium smirked, the moonlight shining on his cheeks and making him look even more like an overfed piglet than he had before. "Nothing will destroy the Grand Resurrection Temple. Nothing except me, and that shall be after I have returned, as Captain Neptune Flannelbottom Bone, to take my place as the New Saviour of the World!"

He threw back his head and laughed gurglingly and loudly, as every follicle of Desdemona's feathers stood on awe-filled end.

The next night, during their out-of-the-Sphinx-wander-through-the-sand-hills-and-collect-the-fresh-food time, Jim, Doris and Brenda beheld the first of the columns that had been erected on the stones of Amehetnehet.

The archaeologist-poet, macaw and Wonder Camel uttered not a word or a snort.

A few hours later, in the early morning, Brenda sneezed within the Great Sphinx of Giza.

She had taken a liking to the disguise that Gerald Perry Esquire had left behind, and she was trying to get the spectacles, false nose and artificial eyebrows and moustache onto her snout, to give Jim and Doris a surprise. This wasn't easy. The disguise lay on the floor in a corner (where it had been accidentally kicked by Jim the day before), and Brenda was having a very hard time trying to retrieve it.

Every time she felt sure she had clamped her teeth onto the spectacles' sidepieces, her snout would get in the way and nudge the disguise further into the corner.

"Quaaooo!" she snorted impatiently.

She felt some dust sniggling into her left nostril. Quickly she raised her head and shook it, around and around. Dust was *not* a welcome visitor.

She lowered her head again, slowly and carefully, bringing her snout as close to the wall as she could. Just when her lips were brushing against the spectacles, another, thicker clump of ancient, gritty dust whooshed into her other nostril.

This time there was no avoiding it.

Brenda lost control, and a sudden, blasting sneeze shot out of both nostrils: "*AAAAAAAAAAHHHHH-HHH-QUUUUAAAAAAAOOOOOOOOOOOOOOO!*"

Jim, who'd been sitting at the table re-reading Bathsheba Snugg's diary, jumped in alarm.

Doris, in her own little macaw-land of dreams, jolted off her perch and into the air.

They looked at their friend, and she blinked her long lashes in embarrassment.

"Are you all right, my lovely?" Jim asked.

"Quaaooo."

And then, from a tiny niche in the wall near where

her head had been when she had sneezed, a small, rolled-up scrap of parchment paper fell to the floor.

It landed on the stones with a small *prapp*. Jim, Doris and Brenda watched it fall and then stared at it.

For almost a minute, nobody moved. A hundred thoughts went through Jim's mind, and his kneecaps tingled with a silent surge of hopefulness and excitement.

Then Doris spoke. "Go on, Jim, pick it up."

Jim went across to the corner and did so.

"Open it, open it," Doris squawked.

He took it over to the table, sat down again, and untied the old brown ribbon that was wound around the parchment. He put the ribbon aside and spread the small square of paper across the table.

Doris hop-fluttered to his shoulder.

Brenda came to be by his side.

Together, silently, they read what was written on the parchment in spidery but neat handwriting.

"Well I'll be a toucan's handbag!" Doris exclaimed.

"Quaaoooo!" said Brenda.

"Swoggle me with somersaults," Jim said. "She came in here!"

"Bathsheba must've written this herself," Doris blinked. "Wouldn't you say, Jim?"

"It's her signature at the bottom. And it's the same handwriting that's in her diary, see?"

They looked at the open page of her diary, then back at the piece of parchment. There was no doubt: it *was* the same handwriting. Jim scratched his chin, then read aloud what was written on the parchment:

> Take 3rd away,
> then add the 7th,
> and then put on the last.
> Then act upon the three of us
> to find the mighty past.
> Bathsheba Snugg

"Rark! What does *that* mean?"

Jim scratched his chin again, then the top of his head, then his left kneecap. "Search me. I'm as confused as a penguin in pyjamas."

Brenda read the message to herself, and bafflement inveigled her mane.

"'Take 3rd away'," Doris muttered, hopping onto the table. "Take 3rd *what* away? And take it away from *where*?"

Jim looked all around the interior of the Sphinx. He went and studied the niche where the parchment had been stuffed. He walked around and up and down the length of the statue, he ran his hands along the limestone walls, but he couldn't see anything that was part of a threesome. "Hmmm."

"Third?" Doris puzzled. "Seventh? What's she – I know! I know what she means!"

"What, Doris?"

"Quaoo quaoo?"

"The seven dwarfs!"

"The what?"

"The seven dwarfs, as in 'Snow White and'! Maybe Bathsheba put a clue in their names."

Jim frowned. "Well, I suppose it's possible. Let's write their names down and see what we come up with. Yes?"

He sat, and for the next ten minutes they tried to remember the names of all the seven dwarfs. But it was useless – Jim and Doris could only recall the first four dwarfs, and Brenda was convinced there was one called Snorty (she told Jim and Doris this through her Wonder Camel telepathy, and Jim added it to the list).

"No," he said, putting down the pencil. "I don't think Snorty's correct. Nor are Sloppy, Stumpy or Patsy. Hmmm. This isn't getting us very far."

Then the bafflement in Brenda's mane shifted and became something else. "Quaoooo!" She implored silently, "Her name! Her name!"

"Rerk!" Doris dug her claws into the tabletop, as Brenda's thought penetrated. "Maybe it's the name!"

"The name?" asked Jim.

"See?" The macaw flexed herself up and down. "She's signed her name there. Bathsheba. Maybe she means her name?"

"You mean the letters in it?"

"Look." She started to read the message again. "'Take 3rd away' ... just say she means the T. That's the third letter in *Bathsheba*."

"Okay." Jim grabbed his pencil and wrote a neat T on his writing pad. "Go on, my dear."

"'Then add the 7th'. B-A-T-H-S-H-E. E! Go on, Jim, write that down!"

He printed an E on the pad, next to the T.

"'And then put on the last'." That's an A, Jim."

Jim wrote A. "'T-E-A'," he read. "Tea?"

"No, not at the moment," Doris said. "This is important."

"No, my dear, look. It spells the word *tea*."

"Tea?"

"Quaaoo?"

Jim read the rest of the message. "'And then act on the three of us to find the mighty past'." That must mean to act on tea."

"Huh?" Doris opened and closed her huge wings. "Act on tea? How do you act on *tea*? I've heard of people acting on the stage, or on the screen, but on *tea*? Gosh, maybe old Bathsheba got a bit addled when she ran away and came here!"

"Act on..." mused Jim. "To act on ... what happens when you act on something? You ... *do* something. Hmmm."

"To do something with tea?" Doris cooed.

"What do you do with tea?" Jim asked.

"Drink it," thought Brenda.

"Drink it," said Doris.

"Then drink tea 'to find the mighty past'. No," Jim shook his head. "I don't think that'll work."

"You slurp tea," said Doris.

Jim looked at her.

"Well, not *you*, Jim, but some people do. Maybe if we make slurping sounds, we might uncover something?"

"What have we got to lose?"

For a few minutes they slurped away on imaginary cups of tea, but all it got them was out of breath, and Brenda began to dribble.

"Okay," Jim said, looking around the Sphinx's interior, "that didn't help much. No hidden doors have been triggered off by our slurps. No false stones or openings or passageways have opened up."

"What else do you do with tea?" asked Doris.

"Brew it," Brenda thought.

"You *brew* it," Jim announced. "Let's try brewing a pot of tea, and see what happens."

"Rerk," rerked Doris.

So Cairo Jim lit the spirit stove and poured some water into the kettle. Quietly the trio watched and waited until the kettle boiled.

"Sweeeeeeeeeehhhh," the kettle whistled urgently after two and a half minutes.

Jim took it off the stove and put it on the floor. Then he added some tea leaves and waited.

Doris and Brenda looked all around the Sphinx's insides.

Nothing. No new revelations at all.

Everything – each piece of limestone, every cobweb, all the nooks and every cranny – remained just as before.

Doris was starting to get flustered. "Rark, rark, rark-a-kark! This is barmy! Here we are with some bit of mystery from the past, and all we're doing is making tea!"

Jim sat in the chair, stumped.

Brenda sniffed the air, to test if anything unusual were about to happen.

Doris fluttered around, her wings itching with frustration. "Well, I guess the next thing is to pour the precious brew."

"Hmm?" Jim blinked. "What'd you say, my dear?"

"Pour it," she repeated. "The tea. Pour, pour, pour!"

"Pour," thought Brenda, letting the word spread into her telepathy cells.

Jim leapt from the chair and grabbed Doris with both hands. "You brilliant, *brilliant* bird!" he cried excitedly.

DEEPER SPHINXING

"WHAT?" DORIS FLAPPED. "What'd I squawk?"

"Only one word," smiled Jim, his eyebrows tingling with hope. "Maybe the one word that Bathsheba wanted us to find."

"Eh?"

"What do we do with the tea now?"

The macaw looked at him strangely. "Well, you can have a bath in it for all I care!"

"No, my dear, what you just said!"

"Pour it!"

"Pour!"

He looked at her, and she at him. Brenda looked at the kettle.

"Say it out loud," Jim said, "without thinking about what it *means*. Listen to how it *sounds*."

"Pour," said the bird.

"Pour," Brenda thought again.

"Now I'll ask you a question, and I want you to answer it with that word."

"Okay, Jim." Doris looked at him strangely.

"What is it that the Sphinx has four of?"

"Pour," Doris answered, and Brenda thought it at the same time.

"Say it again, and listen to the answer."

"Pour. Rark. Pour, pour ... PAW!"

"Quaaooo!"

"That's right." Jim let Doris go, and she flew across the chamber, to the wall where the front left paw started. He and Brenda joined her there. "What if Bathsheba is meaning for us to look in the paws? Maybe there's something in there that'll give us a clue—"

"Why didn't she just say so, then?"

"I think it's because she was a cryptic sort of person," Jim said. He sat on the floor and looked carefully at the paw wall. "She was obviously very secretive; you can tell from the way she rigged up those bookshelves back in the Old Relics Society library. I can understand it, really. Here she was, a clever and solitary type of person, on the verge of making this huge discovery that Herodotitis wrote of."

"Rerk, which we're still in the dark about!"

"Mmm, as was Bathsheba. For a while, anyway. Maybe she deliberately made those clues so strange, so *mysterious,* that if they were found by the wrong type of person, that person wouldn't be able to work out what Bathsheba meant."

"Quaooo," Brenda snorted.

"Perhaps," Jim pondered, "she wanted a certain type of person to follow in her footsteps."

"And camel and macaw," Doris reminded him.

"Of course, Doris. Now, if Bathsheba *did* want us to look in the paws, the question is: which one? Does she mean one of the *front* paws that extend out from under the Sphinx's head, or one of the *back* paws that run along the Sphinx's outsides?"

Doris skimmed the wall of the front left paw. "Let's find out," she squawked. "If we can find a way to get into the paws, that is."

"Hmmm," hmmed Jim. He stood and began to inspect the stones in the front wall, while Doris ran her wingtips delicately across the joins in the stones.

Brenda lumbered over to Jim's knapsack and snouted out his Perspicacious brand archaeological magnifying glass. This she nudged into his hand.

"Thank you, my lovely."

"Quaaoo."

He held the lens close to the limestone, and moved his gaze slowly across the wall. After twenty minutes he stepped back. "No, I don't think there's any sort of opening leading into the front left paw. Can't see any variation in the way the stones have been laid. Let's have a look at the right paw wall."

He and Brenda moved some of their provisions out of the way, so that they could get close to the wall. Again he inspected the stones with his magnifying glass. Doris started to examine the bit of wall above his head.

"Look, here!" Jim pocketed the magnifying glass and ran his fingertips along a groove between two blocks of stone. "This groove is deeper than the others – fractionally, that's all, but deeper for sure. See?"

He traced the groove along the top and down both sides. It bordered an area about half a metre square.

Doris felt the tiny depth with her wingtips. "Rark, you're right!"

Brenda shifted her hoofs on the floor.

"And see the colour of this stone? It's slightly lighter than the other stones in the wall."

"An entrance?" suggested Doris.

"Let's see." Jim knelt in front of the stone. "There's no way I can grip this to pull it out, so maybe we can push it *in*, and then move it a bit to one side. Brenda, my lovely, may I borrow your snout please?"

"Quaaooo." She came in closer and lowered her head until her snout was next to her best human friend. Jim put his palms against the stone, and she put the breadth of her snout against it.

"One, two, three!" Together they pushed hard, Jim's muscles straining and Brenda's nostrils flaring.

"Keep pushing," grunted Jim.

Brenda moved herself so her full weight was behind her snout. With a huge snort, she pressed everything into the job, pushing until both her humps tingled.

"Harder," Jim puffed.

There was a gravelly grinding, and the stone moved.

"Rark, there it goes!"

With a mighty effort, Jim and Brenda pushed the stone into what looked like a narrow passage behind it. A blast of old, hot air shot out at his face and her snout.

"Okay, Brenda, now let's shift it that way, to the left."

They got their hands and snout to the right-hand side of the stone, and nudged it away from the centre of the passageway, until there was just enough room for Jim to squeeze through if he sucked in his breath.

Jim, Brenda and Doris peered into the small passage.

"Too dark," Doris screeched. "Hang on a mo!" She shot off and fetched their three torches from under Jim's stretcher. These she winged to her friends, placing Jim's into his hand and Brenda's into her jaws.

As one, Jim, Doris and Brenda flicked on the torches (Brenda had a dexterous Wonder Camel tongue) and pointed the beams of light into the passage.

"Look," Jim whispered, his beam travelling slowly up and away to the right. "It ascends. Steeply, by the look of it."

The narrow passage disappeared away from them, upwards and darkly, into a murkiness their torches could not fathom.

"Quaooo," snorted Brenda, worried by the uncertainty of where the passage might lead.

"It seems to be going back, into the top of the Sphinx," observed Jim. "Somewhere over our heads. It's steep, but not impossible."

"Jim," Doris said, "let me go and have a look. It's very narrow in there, and I could easily fly up and turn around to come back if I have to."

"I'm sure I could as well, my dear," he said, trying to shine his beam as high as it could go before the blackness smothered it. "Climb, I mean, not fly."

"Yes, yes, but I'll be quicker. Just in case I have to get away from anything unpleasant or dangerous."

Brenda nodded her head in a circular motion – she thought there was good sense in Doris's reckoning.

"All right, my dear." He moved back a little way from the opening, and she stepped into the passage, peering up.

"You're being exceptionally brave, Doris," Jim said, reaching out and patting her crest gently. "I know how much you hate small enclosed spaces."

She took a big gulp and cleared her little throat. "Comes a time when a macaw has to forget about herself and go onwards, if only for the sake of History," she said, and Jim felt an enormous glow of pride and admiration for her. "And anyway," she added, "I really want to know what that cryptic old gal Snugg was up to!"

"See you soon," Jim said. "Try not to be more than a few minutes, otherwise I'll come in after you."

"Rightio."

Brenda thought, "Good luck, my small friend."

"Thanks, Bren." Doris blinked. "Now why did I say that, I wonder? Never mind, see you in two shakes of a camel's tail!" She put her torch in her beak, balanced it carefully and then, with small, cramped beats of her wings, she slowly flew up and into the gloom.

Jim and Brenda watched as her outline became dull, until the shine of her feathers was finally swallowed up by the darkness, and all that could be seen was the beam from her torch. Gradually that, too, became fainter. Then it faded completely. And all up there was black.

Jim reached out and rubbed Brenda's snout. "She'll be all right. Don't worry, my lovely," he said, his voice small but steady.

"Quaooo."

For several minutes they waited, listening so hard they thought their ears would fall off. But no sound came from up there – no beating of wings, no small stones or powdery sand falling, no wind or air currents.

Brenda shook her tail twice, to try and test what Doris had said, but it was no good – Doris wasn't back by the time Brenda's tail had stopped shaking. The Wonder Camel snorted worriedly.

"Yes, Brenda, good idea. I'll give her a call." Jim crawled a few paces into the passageway and cupped his hands around his mouth. "Doris?"

His voice sounded flat and hollow as it smacked back off the narrow stone walls.

Silence.

"Doris? My dear, are you there?"

More silence, so big it was almost deafening in a strange and prickling way.

"I'm going after her," he said, his eyes clouded. "She might be stuck."

"Quaooo." Brenda quickly stood and fetched Jim's pith helmet. She snouted it to him.

"Thanks, you Wonder. You know how I don't like to go off into the unknown without it."

He put it on, fastened the chin-strap under his chin, and turned to face the rising tunnel. "I'll be back soon. Hold the fort, or should I say the *Sphinx*, till then."

She rolled her head and snorted.

He started to climb, being helped for the first metre by Brenda's snout pushing against his shorts.

The passage was hot and the air within was stale. Jim slowly moved upwards, using his free hand to grip onto the wall to the left of him. The wall was rough, and he was able, here and there, to grip onto rocks jutting out.

The floor beneath was sandy and gritty. The higher he climbed, the less compacted the floor became, and after a minute his boots slid away from under him as small rocks and sand clods showered down from beneath his soles.

He grabbed a large rock in the wall, steadied himself, and waited for a moment, holding his breath, until the dust from the grit-shower had settled. Shining his torchbeam down the passage, he watched as the dust danced about in the thick darkness.

Then he shone the beam upwards again, and got on with the climb.

Up, up, hotly up he climbed and skidded, his shirt starting to cling to his back, his hair becoming damp under his pith helmet. The higher he went, the more spindly the light from his torch became. Soon it was nothing more than a pin-prick in the impenetrable murkiness.

He stopped and took a deep breath, wiping some fine sand from his forehead. The passage was getting steeper here, and the floor was very unstable. Tilting back his hat, he continued.

And smacked hard against a wall in front of him.

"Ouch!" He rubbed his chin, shining the torch on his hand afterwards. No blood, at least. He was sure he'd have a huge bruise tomorrow.

He felt the wall with his hand. A dead end?

Is this where the passage finished?

Then where was Doris?

He looked to the right, trying to illuminate the gloom. At the edges of his torchbeam he saw, further on, that the passage continued along at a right-angle to where he was. Steeply, as before.

He turned and followed this new section. On, on and on, upwards all the time, the sand moving under his boots, his torch offering barely any help at all.

And then ...

       suddenly...

              he came to another wall, seeing it before hitting it with his chin, and, quicker than it takes to blink, a bright shaft of light jumped out at him.

He turned to the left and saw that the light was coming from a hole in a wall, about five metres ahead. Turning off his torch, he moved towards it, walking carefully up the sloping floor.

"Doris?" he called. "My dear?"

No answer.

He pocketed the torch and moved closer to the hole. It was a little under half as big as him. He knelt before it and looked through.

Daylight!

Daylight? he wondered.

He crouched closer to the hole, so that he could move his head to the opening.

Without warning, the floor beneath gave way, swinging off and back to the centre of the passageway, and Cairo Jim went spilling through the hole headfirst with a great cry of astonishment!

Off into the unknown!

19

THE TEMPLE OF MR IMPLUVIUM

BRENDA WAS WORRIED.

It had been a long time now since Jim had followed Doris up the passageway, and the Wonder Camel had heard neither squawk nor footstep.

She craned her neck as far into the passage as she could and looked up, lighting the passage with her torch. But there was nothing to see, except for a gloomy murkiness which her torchbeam grappled weakly with.

She pulled her head out and sat, cross-legged, on the floor of the Sphinx. Where were they? Why hadn't they returned?

"Quaooo," she snorted, as she spied Gerald Perry Esquire's disguise next to her. She picked it up with her snout and started to put it on. Distractions such as these were very welcome under the current circumstances...

Meanwhile, the vast Resurrection Temple of Bonelaten was slowly taking shape above the stones of Amehetnehet.

Neptune Bone leant back against one of the two thousand columns that Desdemona had super-glued along the northern perimeter of the limestone slabs.

He dabbed at his sweaty forehead with his handkerchief, and puffed heavily on his cigar.

"Arrr. That's about it for the outside columns."

"Are you sure you've got enough?" asked Desdemona, perched above him like a ghastly feathered gargoyle. Around her skull, and clamped to the edges of her beak, was a squirty-gun in which was secured the large tube of extra-strength super-glue.

"Oh, yes, we don't want to overdo it. The columns are merely the *simple* adornments, the outside things that visitors will see first. Now we have to put all of the *detailed* bits and pieces inside."

The raven looked back at the truck full of Spiffystone carvings, and then eyeballed him again.

"Next," he continued, exhaling the cigar smoke through his chimney-like nostrils, "I shall position those arches above the columns. All seventeen hundred of them. And then we shall add the sixty-five ziggurats, the nineteen Contemplation Wells, the three Holy of Holies Chambers, the nine altars of Pharaoh Bonelaten, the Eternal After Life Fountains and the Raised Promenade of Enlightenment—"

"How about a couple of kitchen sinks?"

"Shut it, slimewings. And finally, the piece of resistance: the Most Hallowed Resurrection Prediction Wall, which shall be plonked in the exact centre of Amehetnehet's stones." He inspected a fingernail, and rubbed it fussily against his galabiyya. "I shall invite the press to the unveiling of that," he declared importantly.

Desdemona's eyes throbbed at him in a mixture of awe and mockery. "Just what are your *dreams* like?"

He sucked in the smoke and poured it out into the hot desert air. "I live my dreams every day," he purred in a thick and pillowy voice. "And the greatest dream of all is yet to come. Arrrrrrrrrrrrr!"

Above, in the clear blue sky, Doris gave a piercing screech. "REEEEEEEEERRRAAAAAARRRRRRKKKKK!"

"Doris!" cried Jim, his fingernails digging into the limestone, his legs dangling helplessly above the ground so far below. "Where am I?"

She swooped, and hovered close by his shoulder. "Steady on, Jim, you're hanging from the Sphinx's left nostril cavity!"

He looked down. Far below, the front paws of the Sphinx stretched out across the sand. If he fell from here, he probably wouldn't live to write another poem. Terrified, he kicked his feet this way and that, but he couldn't find a foothold above the mighty statue's mouth.

The limestone began crumbling under his fingernails.

He stopped kicking and tried to get his kneecap back up into the nostril cavity. A chunk of rock fell onto his shoulder.

He shot his left hand across, to what he hoped was a safer bit of the cavity. As his fingers closed around the rock ledge a small section broke away, crashing onto his pith helmet.

"Doris, help!"

His left hand slipped, and he found himself holding on by only three fingers of his other hand. Tiny streams of perspiration were dribbling down his fingers, and his hand started to slide towards the Sphinx's mouth.

"Whoooooaaahhhh! Doris, I'm falling!"

"Here!" She flew down and then up, until she was under his leg. With as much strength as she could muster, she bumped his leg higher and higher, until his knee was on the ledge of the nostril cavity.

"Clamber back in, Jim," she screamed, bumping him with her wings.

He didn't know how, but he managed to get most of his leg back into the nostril cavity. Then he humped his lower torso in after it, and then his other leg and his chest. Finally his head was all that was sticking out of the hole.

"Wish I had a camera," Doris said.

"Come on back inside," Jim puffed. "I've had enough of dead ends!"

Later, when Jim and Doris had slid and fluttered back down the passageway to be greeted by a spectacled, moustached and strangely eyebrowed Brenda, they decided to try one of the back paws.

Brenda, who had an eye for such things, sent out a thought: "With tea, you pour from the left. The left back paw has a small slab of rock that protrudes from the rest. Look."

"Rark," Doris rarked suddenly. "Look! The left back paw has a small slab of rock that protrudes from the rest."

"So it does," Jim observed.

"Quaaaooo," said Brenda.

"And because this is sticking a little way out," Jim said, gripping the outermost edges of the slab, "we might be able to pull it, instead of having to push it like that other one."

Squatting before the slab, he dug his fingers in as hard as he could, and took the strain. Then he leaned back and pulled.

Slowly, with a grinding of rock on rock, the slab moved back towards him.

"A bit more, Jim," Doris instructed as she hover-fluttered above the slab. "Just a little … there! There's room now!"

A square opening was revealed, dark and shadowy. Jim let go of the slab and took a swig of water from his water bottle. "Let's have a look," he whispered.

They crowded the entrance, each of them peering in.

Ahead was a corridor. Doris shone her torch into it.

"It goes down," Jim said. "Unlike the other one. Suits me – I don't fancy dangling from any more nostrils today!"

"Rark, feel the air!"

A cool, stale current of air wafted gently against them.

"That's a welcome change from the other one, too," Jim said. "Cool, not hot. Doris, shine your torch onto the ground in there."

She did so. The floor of the corridor swept down and away, littered with small rocks and what looked like flat, smooth, pale pieces of something-or-other.

"Quaaooo?" snorted Brenda.

"Jim!" Doris whispered. "Could those flat bits be *plaster*?"

Cairo Jim's heart beat three paces quicker. His eyes followed the yellow torchbeam across the pieces on the floor. "That they could," he answered in a voice of restrained excitement. "If they are, it means that humans have been down here."

Doris's feathers stood on end. Brenda's mane bristled.

Jim got his torch and knapsack. "Right," he said, checking that all three of their water bottles were filled, and that his necessary archaeological equipment was secure in the knapsack, "it looks like there's enough room down there for all of us. Do you both want to come?"

"Do bees buzz?" asked Doris.

"Do sloths sleep?" thought Brenda with a snort.

"Good." Jim strapped down the knapsack and hoisted it over his shoulder. "I always like it when we're all together. Let's go then, carefully and lightly."

Doris gave Brenda and Jim their torches, and together they crept into the hole.

Jim went first, with Doris waddling close to his ankles and Brenda crouching in the rear. Jim shone his torch up at the ceiling.

"Look," he said. "It's high enough for me to stand up in here. So can you, Brenda, if you keep your head low."

He rose, and so did Brenda.

Doris lit the corridor ahead. "Looks like it'll be high enough for some time," she cooed. "And wide enough for me to fly. Not fully stretched, wing-wise, though."

"Downwards and onwards, then," breathed the archaeologist-poet.

They moved ahead and down. The floor was stable enough, but Jim and Brenda still had to be careful where they put their feet and hoofs – sometimes, as they ventured on, Brenda's back legs would skid a little, and once, Jim almost went pith helmet over heels when he momentarily lost his footing.

The air grew more chilly the further they descended. It was still fresh enough to breathe, however. Every now and then, a small gust would dance past them, darting across the hairs above Jim's knees, over Doris's crest feathers and into Brenda's nostrils.

Halfway down, Jim stopped and shone his light on the floor. He stooped and picked up a piece of the flat, smooth something-or-other.

He turned it over delicately in his hands. "It's plaster, all right," he whispered, as Doris and Brenda looked closely. "See the colour?"

"Rark. Light orange."

"Light, but bright," Jim observed. "The orange paint hasn't faded, I'd say. This is probably the exact same tone that was painted soon after the plaster was laid."

"When do you think that might've been?" blinked Doris.

Jim sniffed it. "Hard to tell, without my dating equipment. It *smells* old – sweet and forgotten and dusty – but I couldn't be sure for the moment. Maybe a few thousand years, maybe not." He shone his beam across the walls. "There! See? There're still bits of the plaster sticking to the walls. That's where it came from."

Onwards they continued, skidding sometimes and faltering, while Doris fluttered on ahead. After a few minutes, Jim and Brenda heard her voice. It was quiet but excited.

"Coo. Down here, you two. Look what I've found."

Jim and Brenda clambered down the last few metres to join her. She was perched on a narrow shelf that had been carved into the wall. Next to her, on the shelf, stood an old lantern, thick with dust.

"Where d'you reckon *this* came from?" asked Doris.

Jim took it from the shelf and rubbed it. "It's not ancient. The brass is modern. Wait, here's something written underneath." He shone his torch directly onto the underside of the lantern, and read out loud: "Property of B. Snugg. Keep your hands off if you know what's good...' hmmm. The rest has gone."

"She *was* here!" Doris screeched.

"Shhh," my dear, cautioned Jim. "We don't want to upset the rock around us with any loud noises."

"My apologies," she said, much more quietly.

"Quaaoo," Brenda snorted. She was standing further down, against the wall, and was balancing on her two back legs and pointing with her two front hoofs.

Jim put the lantern back on the shelf and he and Doris hurried to the Wonder Camel.

"Quaaaoooo," she snorted again, moving her front hoofs to the left and right.

Jim's light shone to the left, and Doris's to the right.

"You clever beast of Wonder," Jim smiled, the hairs on the back of his neck standing on end.

"Good one, Bren," Doris cooed, her tailfeathers stiffening.

Brenda was directing them to two narrow doorways carved into the stone wall. From beyond these doorways, a darkness that was much thicker, much deeper, much more cool and uncertain, was shimmering.

"Let's look in this one first," Jim whispered, creeping carefully to the left door. He shone his light into the gloom. The beam scanned across three roughly finished walls covered in bits of the orange plaster.

"Looks like a room. A room that hasn't been used for anything," he said quietly. He slowly craned his head through the door, looking upwards in case there was a trap (or an 'Exploration Deterrent', as many archaeologists called them) above the doorway.

"*CRRRRRAAAARRRRRRRRKKKKKKK!*" Doris screamed, flying back onto Brenda's fore hump.

Jim jumped and banged his pith helmet on the top of the doorway. "Doris, what—?"

Her feathers were trembling. "Th-th-there," she stammered, her torchbeam shaking uncontrollably all over the place. "On the fl-fl-floor. Look!"

Jim and Brenda peered into the room, running their lights across the floor.

"Quaaooo!" Brenda reared, and Jim grabbed her mane and brought her steadily down again.

The floor before them was littered with bones – dozens of small, yellowing, broken-down bones and tiny skulls. Some of the skulls were staring up, hollow-eyed, toothless, grinning.

"Bats," said Jim. "Ancient bats. Flew in here long ago and couldn't get out again."

"Yeerrrgh." Doris shuddered.

Jim cast his light across the small room once more. "Let's look in the other room," he said. "If there's nothing in there, we'll come back to this one and have a closer look."

Doris shuddered again.

The room on the right was bigger, and the gloom within was thicker. Great curtains of cobwebs hung tattily from the ceiling, wafting in the breeze.

Together, the trio shone their lights around the orange plastered walls.

"Feel that breeze," Jim whispered, as the cool gusts

blew about his face. "I'd say this room is only an entrance to somewhere beyond, somewhere that goes even deeper—"

"Quaooo!" Something had been lit by Brenda's torch. "Rark, Jim, look!"

Jim swept his beam across the room, to the spot where Brenda's beam was resting: a low recess carved into the right wall, in the shape of a bed.

"Bathsheba," he whispered, his voice smothered by the dust and the cobwebs and the sight that lay ahead.

20

BATHSHEBA'S LAST CLUE

THERE, ON THE BED-LIKE LEDGE carved into the rock, as still as an unspoken word, lay the figure of a woman.

She was on her side, her left arm tucked up so that her hand formed a natural pillow under her head. Her long, dark hair was spread across her shoulder and down her back, and her eyes were closed. She was wearing a black skirt and frilly white blouse. Below her, placed neatly on the floor, was a pair of pointy red boots.

"Bathsheba," Jim whispered again, as he cast his beam slowly across the still figure.

"Is she sleeping?" asked Doris.

The torchbeam picked out a tiny, intricate network of wispy lines, criss-crossing this way and that, covering her body and binding her to the stone ledge beneath. "Not under all those cobwebs she isn't," said Jim. "At least, it's not the sleep of the living."

He walked slowly into the room, followed by Doris and Brenda. Together they beheld the beautifully preserved Bathsheba Snugg.

"See how young she still is," Jim said quietly. "She must have died shortly after she came in here.

Some time soon after she disappeared, back in 1908."

"'We are such stuffs as dreams are made of, and our little life is rounded with a sleep,'" Doris quoted from *The Tempest*.

"This is her sepulchre," Jim said. "The place where she wanted to lay herself to rest. And its cool, dry conditions have preserved her – as though she's only asleep."

"She looks more calm than the Pharaohs and the Queens in the Cairo Museum," observed Doris.

"Even the ancient Egyptians would be envious of this natural embalming process."

"Quaaooo," snorted Brenda, moving her beam urgently back and forth near Bathsheba's clenched hand.

Jim caught sight of what she was highlighting. "Yes, my lovely! Look, Doris, it's a scroll!"

"Rark."

Jim leant down and carefully broke through the old, dusty cobweb-blanket. He gently prised the parchment scroll from Bathsheba's hand. "Perry was right," he said, unrolling the parchment. "She *did* take it with her that day."

Doris squinted at the writing on the scroll. "Ancient Greek," she announced. "Looks like it's Herodotitis."

Jim handed her the scroll and dumped his knapsack on the floor. He rummaged round inside and took out Bathsheba's diary. Opening it to the bookmarked page, he held the entry for June third, 1908, next to the scroll.

"There," he said. "The original, and the translation. Herodotitis is describing the Greatest Wonder ever ... the monument so brilliantly built that it defies explanation."

"'More marvellous, more astonishing, more breath-takingly, ambitiously and stunningly built, than all of the Seven Wonders of the World put together'," Doris read.

"I wonder," Jim said to Bathsheba's body, "whether you got any closer to it than we did..."

And then the brilliant Wonder Camel saw something else, and gave a *quaaaoooo* of great importance.

"What, Bren? What've you found this time?" Doris shone her torch at Brenda's face (Brenda still had on the glasses and artificial eyebrows and moustache), then to the spot where Brenda was trying to draw their attention.

"Huh?" said Jim, lighting up Bathsheba's big toe on her right foot.

"Her toe?" asked Doris.

Brenda moved her snout close to the cobwebs covering the toe, and then jerked her head away to the right. "Look," she thought. "The toe isn't in a natural position. Bathsheba's deliberately bent it that way. She's pointing at something."

Her thought rose, mingled with the cool, dry air for a second, and shot straight into Doris's head.

"Rark! I know what Brenda's getting at. Bathsheba's toe isn't in a natural position. She's deliberately bent it that way. She's pointing at something!"

Brenda drew an imaginary line from Bathsheba's lilac-painted toenail to the right wall. She moved her head along this line, and the beam from the torch in her mouth shimmered through the room, coming to rest on a tall, narrow slit in the wall.

"A slit," Doris squawked.

"We couldn't see it in those shadows," Jim said. He looked from Bathsheba's toenail to the slit and back again. "I guess she *was* pointing." He led Doris and Brenda to the slit.

It was wide enough at the ground for Jim to be able to wriggle through, and Brenda also, if she sucked in her humps. As the slit rose towards the ceiling, it tapered away to a crumbled point.

They shone their torches through the opening. A steep shaft, almost perpendicular, disappeared down into the gloom.

"Brrrr," Doris shivered. "It's colder down there."

Jim lit up both sides of the shaft walls. "How wide d'you reckon it is?"

Doris looked for a few moments. "About three metres," she answered. "Up near this entrance, at least. We can't see very far down there, even with these torches."

"Big enough for Brenda to come with us," Jim murmured.

"Quaaaooo?"

"Don't worry, Brenda, we'll all be together."

"Rark. How are you two supposed to go down? Plummet?"

"Plummet?"

"It's so steep. There's no way you and Bren could

walk. It'd be more dangerous than walking down the highest face of Mount Everest in ballet slippers."

Jim kept shining his light around the shaft.

"I, of course," Doris went on, "I can *fly* down. We birds were designed for exploration much more sensibly than you two-legs and four-legs. We can flutter into nooks and crannies that you couldn't even dream about."

"See those pegs? *That's* how Brenda and I'll go down," said Jim.

On both walls at either side of the shaft, a sequence of short, thick wooden pegs was protruding.

"See?" Jim whispered. "Each of those thick timber pegs is spaced at such a distance from the one above it that Brenda and I should be able to use them as foot- and hoof-rungs. We can go down as if we're descending two ladders that are opposite each other."

To show Brenda what he meant, he shone his torch on the first peg on the left wall, then at the second peg on the right wall, then back to the third peg on the left wall. "See, my lovely, there, and there, and there. Like rungs on opposite ladders."

Brenda gave a timid snort – climbing ladders was not amongst her favourite pastimes. In fact, she avoided doing so whenever possible.

"Don't worry," Jim rubbed her snout reassuringly, "it won't be any harder than those pyramids in Mexico."

She fluttered her eyelashes and felt a bit better.

"What about you, Doris? There's enough space between all those pegs for you to fly down, but the shaft *is* enclosed. Will you be okay?"

She puffed out her chestfeathers and gave him a brave wink. "Standing on the verge of what might be the greatest historical discovery of the millennium, am I going to let a little thing like claustrophobia dampen my feathers? You bet your ink bottles I won't!"

"What friends I have," smiled the archaeologist-poet. "Now, let's go. You first, Doris, then Brenda. I'll bring up the rear. And one thing: go slowly and be ever-vigilant, because we might be about to find something important. And, if we *do* find something, perhaps the something that led Bathsheba here, remember what Herodotitis said: 'Tread carefully... Greatness such as this is easily toppled.'"

"Rightio," said Doris. "I'll land on the pegs as I go down, to make sure there aren't any rotten ones." She clamped her torch in her beak, leant forward and, like a diver entering a pool of water, let herself fall into the shaft. With a constrained beating of wings, she and her light descended into the darkness.

"Go on, my lovely," Jim said to Brenda. He took her spectacles, false nose, moustache and fake eyebrows from her snout and put them in his knapsack, along with Bathsheba's diary and Herodotitis's scroll. "I'm right behind."

She gave a small snort and went to the opening. Carefully she lowered her back legs, until her left hoof was on the first peg on the left wall. Then her right hoof felt about in mid-air until it found the second peg on the opposite wall.

This peg gave a shrill creak as she stood on it.

Slowly she moved her left hoof down – it seemed like she was moving it through all of Eternity, and she thought she would never be able to find the next left-wall peg. But eventually she did, and as her hoof settled on the peg, she made a mental note of the distance between each peg. This would, she hoped, help her as she went down.

Slowly the Wonder Camel disappeared into the shaft.

Jim secured his knapsack, adjusted his pith helmet, and, with his heart beating as though a cyclone was blowing around in his ribcage, he started climbing down as well.

The shaft kept sweeping away, into what Jim imagined were the very bowels of the earth. The further the trio descended, the cooler the air became, and the silence – a silence Jim had only encountered in long-forgotten, ancient places where no one had been for centuries – was echoing and eerie.

After a while of descending, he spoke: "You know what we're in?"

"What?" Doris asked quietly over her wing.

"Quaaoo?" asked Brenda, her right hoof in mid-air.

"A Workers' Shaft. I've read about these, but've never been in one until now. They were very common

in great buildings of the Fourth Dynasty."

"A Workers' Shaft?" Doris said.

"Mm-hm. Built to allow the last of the workers – the ones who put the final stones of a building in place – a way to get out. Workers' Shafts were necessary when the builders didn't want people to know where the entrances and exits to the buildings were. The workers could come and go through these shafts, often emerging at a place that was miles from where the building actually stood."

He continued following Brenda downwards, while Doris fluttered ahead, but still within earshot. "It's easy to tell this is a Workers' Shaft because of the pegs. The workers used to climb up, in the same way that we're going down. We haven't found any other sorts of ancient shafts where these timber pegs were used. There's something else about these shafts, something I read a while ago. What was it?"

He kept descending, being careful not to drop his torch as he gripped the pegs above him while he lowered his legs to the pegs below.

Suddenly the full force of memory came rushing into his brain, and his face turned chalk-pale.

"What was it you read?" Doris asked as she perched on a peg a little way below Brenda. "Can you remember?"

"Let's keep going, gang. We don't want to waste—"

GGGGRRRRRREENNNNHHHHHKKKKKK!

"Rark!" Doris jumped off the peg. "What was that?"

"Quaaoooo!"

"That sound," the macaw squawked. "Didn't you hear it? It came from up there!"

Beads of perspiration dotted Jim's brow. "Probably just the ground above shifting a little. Those desert sands are always on the move."

GGGGRRRRREENNNNHHHHHKKKKKK!

The sound came again, but not as loud this time.

"Let's keep moving," said Jim urgently.

Doris flew off, and Brenda started lowering herself more quickly. There was something in Jim's tone that suggested she should not dilly-dally.

"Rark! That's funny."

"What's funny, Doris?"

GGGGRRRRREENNNNHHHHHKKKKKK!

Fainter again this time.

"The lower I fly, the harder it is to stretch my wings. Yet a few minutes ago, everything looked like it was the same width all the way down."

The perspiration was running freely down into Jim's eyebrows, and onwards.

"*The walls!*" Brenda thought, her tail sticking out with panic. "*The walls are moving inwards!*"

"REERRAAAAARRKKK! Jim, the walls are moving inwards!"

"I hoped this wouldn't happen – this is what I remembered from my reading! Workers' Shafts were always booby trapped so that no one could enter! We must be the first ones to come down here, since—"

"*Hurry!*" screeched Doris, *"before we're squashed to death!"*

"Quick," Jim shouted, "down, down, DOWN!"

Steadily, with grinding determination, the walls were closing in. Small clods of rock and earth started falling from above.

Whooooooosh!

Splintering, cracking pegs flew into the shaft like arrows.

"Hurry! Brenda, my lovely, don't stop! Concentrate! Look where you're putting your hoofs!"

The pegs under Brenda's hoofs slid inwards, bit by bit. She had to judge the distance for each peg anew, because every time she took a hoof off one peg, the peg below was closer to the opposite peg than before, and she had to spread her limbs less each time.

"I'm going ahead," Doris screeched, "to see if there's an ending in sight!"

"Fly, Doris, but come back!"

She shot off, dodging the encroaching pegs and the clods of falling rock and splinters of wood. Her light disappeared into the contracting space ahead.

Brenda kept descending. The pegs were getting closer and closer. Now she found that she didn't have to stretch her legs very widely at all: for a few moments, the pegs were spaced naturally for her stance. But the walls were not stopping, and the shaft was narrowing and narrowing.

"Brenda!" Jim yelled down. "You'll have to compress

yourself! Snort out every last little bit of air. The pegs will be pressing soon! Deflate your humps as much as you can!"

"*Quaaoo!*" She exhaled deeply, pushing out great gulps of air from her belly. Her sides compacted, like an accordion's, and she continued quickly downwards.

Clack-ta-clack-ta-clack went her hoofs on the pegs.

Jim's sweating hands were almost slipping off the pegs to the left and right of him, and his trembling Sahara boots barely touched the pegs below as he scrambled down like a distressed spider.

Then the build-up of moisture on his palms turned into a torrent of perspiration, and his torch slid from his grip and fell.

Down, down, crashingly down it went, narrowly missing Brenda's humps, clattering loudly against the pegs as it bounced across one way and then across the other. It kept falling, coming closer and closer to Doris.

"Doris!" shouted Jim. "Watch out!"

But it was too late – she turned her head towards him, and the torch bounced off a peg to her left and hit her hard behind her crest.

With not even a moment to make a sound, her eyes closed, she dropped her torch, and down she plummeted, her wings limp as she corkscrewed through the shaft.

"NO!" Jim cried. He and Brenda paused, and watched until the darkness smothered up her still body.

Now the walls were gaining momentum, pushing in harder, faster, more menacingly. Brenda had barely enough room to angle herself as she almost slid down. The pegs had started to dig sharply into her sides, and her long eyelashes were drenched with terror.

"Brenda, there's nothing for it now!" The sweat was running down into Jim's eyes, the salt stinging. "In a minute there won't be any room between the pegs to squeeze ourselves. We have to let go and fall through the gaps!"

"*Quuuaaaoooo!*" she snorted. She knew he was right, even if it did mean something terrible happening to them. It was that, or death by a thousand spearing pegs.

"One, two, THREE! LET GO NOW MY LOVELY!"

She took her four hoofs off the pegs, raised her front legs above her snout, and pointed her back legs straight down. As more clods of rock fell around her, she slipped down the shaft, her torch raised high to light the way for Jim above.

Jim pulled his hands and legs away and hurtled after her like a human torpedo. As he sped down he saw the pegs above him moving in faster – the ones lit up by Brenda's torch were splintering loudly against each other.

Down through the barely lit shaft they fell, scraping their limbs against the rough pegs that were encroaching like silent batons of mortality.

As he tumbled and fell, Jim kept his eyes open for Doris, but there was no sign of her.

And then, with a loud grunt, Brenda hit a flat surface. She pulled in her legs, bent them under her, and rolled into a big space that was away from the shaft.

"OOOFFFFFF!" gasped Jim, the air knocked out of his lungs as he, too, hit the ground. He looked around, and saw the motionless bundle of feathers that was Doris. Quickly, as the pegs on either side of his head started to touch his temples, he swept the macaw up.

"Quaaaoooo!" came Brenda's urgent snort. "It's safe over here! HURRY!"

Jim bundled Doris into his shirt and scrambled so fast that he was a blur against the shaft's walls. He skidded to Brenda's side as the shaft closed off completely.

TTHHHHHHHNNNNNNNNNKKKKKKKKKK!

Now there was silence, a silence broken only by the faint sound of settling dust and grit, and the groaning of the deep earth surrounding them.

Gently, tenderly, Jim took Doris from his shirt and laid her on the floor of the small room they were in.

"Quaaooo?" A large, heavy tear welled up in the Wonder Camel's eye. She inhaled deeply, and, as her sides inflated to their normal width, it seemed that she was breathing in all the sorrow of the world.

"It's all right, Brenda," he soothed. "See? Her little chest is moving. She's just unconscious, that's all."

He slung off his knapsack and took out his water bottle from it. With shaking fingers, he sprinkled big, fat droplets across Doris's beak and eyes and crest.

The brave bird blinked her small eyes and opened them. She moved her beak up and down, as if she were wearing it for the very first time and she was getting used to the fit. Then she saw the slightly out-of-focus figures above her.

Her vision cleared and she said, in her bossy macaw's voice: "Well, it's about time you two showed up. What'd you do – stop for a picnic?"

The bruised archaeologist-poet and the bruised Wonder Camel laughed and snorted with such relief that they felt quite giddy.

"So?" said Doris, getting up and waddling round the small room. She peered at the dead-end wall that was all that was left of the shaft. "We can't go back that way, unless we're moles. What now?"

"Through there, I suppose," Jim answered, pouring some water over Brenda.

Doris picked up her torch – miraculously, it hadn't broken when she had dropped it. She aimed the beam into the dark opening at the opposite end of the room. "Rerark! Looks like a tunnel."

"I'd bet my pith helmet it leads to the building that the Workers' Shaft was protecting." Jim stood and packed the water bottle away. He looked at the sealed shaft, and then turned to face the tunnel. His heart was heavy yet hopeful. "Come on," he whispered, "let's find this ancient destiny of ours!"

21

CORNERSTONE IN PLACE?

ABOVE THE TUNNEL, and considerably to the east, the person formerly known to the world as Captain Neptune Flannelbottom Bone was erecting the last of his Spiffystone pieces on the exact centre of the Amehetnehet slabs.

Desdemona watched him through slitted, throbbing eyes as he pulled on the rope that was tied around an enormous wall-section containing a huge inscription carved inside an ornate cartouche.

"I hope," she whined wearily, "that that's the last of all of this. Sheesh! This super-glue gun has been strapped to me skull for so long, it feels like it's started to *grow* there!"

Mr Impluvium pushed the wall onto the centre slabs. "Fear not, you treacherous tool of tediousness, this *is* the last piece. The Most Hallowed Resurrection Prediction Wall. The cornerstone of my whole enterprise. The piece that will allow me to sashay forth into the world once again, only this time, whole nations will bow and grovel to me. Which is just as it should have always been. Arrrr."

The raven plonked herself heavily on the floor and looked at her surroundings: the thousands of

Spiffystone arches and columns and fountains and altars and Contemplation Wells and vestibules and ziggurats and colonnades and sphinxettes and all the rest, every single piece of lightweight sculpture glistening brilliantly in the strong sunshine. She turned her beady glare back to her companion. "What's so special about this bit, then? What's this got going for it that'll change your destiny?"

Impluvium sucked on his cigar and shoved the piece of wall firmly into place. "My entire Genius is on this piece," he answered smugly. "Quite possibly the greatest, most daring and audaciously bold scheme I have ever dreamt up."

"Eh?"

"Look, you mutant feather-duster. See what is written in this cartouche? A proclamation. I had that Sozan chappie carve it to my instructions, in ancient hieroglyphics."

"A proclamation?"

"Arrr. A proclamation that will herald my return from the dead, my resurrection, so that I shall have the world stretched before me. I shall stride it like a colossus, and be able to amass all the gold, diamonds, silver and Belch of Brouhaha cigars on the planet, all for myself. Not to mention wiping out all those infernal rainforests and jungles, which as you know I have always felt to be the most sinister places anywhere!"

"What's this proclamation say, then?"

"Let me translate it for you." He took the cigar from his mouth and flourished it in the air as his eyes followed the hieroglyphics and his flabby lips gave them sound. "Ahem:

'THIS KNOWLEDGE SHALL BE IMPARTED TO THOSE WHO HAVE FOUND THEIR WAY TO THIS, THE HOLIEST OF HOLIES. BE IT KNOWN THAT THERE SHALL COME, BACK FROM THE AFTER LIFE TO WALK AGAIN ON THE EARTH, ONE WHO SHALL LEAD ALL MEN, WOMEN AND EVERYONE ELSE; ONE WHO SHALL BE KNOWN AS THE RULER OF THE WORLD, THE NEW SAVIOUR OF THE WORLD, THE GREATEST OF GODS AND FASHION LEADERS. HE IS A DESCENDANT OF MINE, AND I AM THE IMMORTAL PHARAOH BONELATEN. HIS NAME SHALL BE NEPTUNE FLANNELBOTTOM BONK.'"

"Bonk?" said Desdemona. "Ha-crark-ha-crark-haaarrrr!"

"Don't be so rude," Bone sneered.

"No," she spluttered, "you just read it out!"

"I most certainly did no—" He saw the end of the proclamation again and his shaven cheeks turned beetroot red. "AAARRRRR! Curse that stupid stonemason. One slip of the chisel and eternal reverence flies out the window!"

"What now, Captain Bonk?"

"Shut your flea-infested gob." He puffed furiously on his cigar, then grabbed the super-glue gun from Desdemona's head.

"Ouch!" she winced.

"A little dab of this stuff on the offending hieroglyph, and – there we go – it looks like a blemish of age upon the Spiffystone. A bit of weathering from ancient times. Now, it looks like it could very well read 'Bone'."

"Any room there to add a bit about how this New Saviour of the World will be assisted by a dashing, glossy raven who emanates wisdom and brilliant thoughts?"

"No," he answered coldly.

"Ratso."

"And even if I had time to add such a bit of nonsense, I would hardly bother." He reached in under his galabiyya and pulled out his gold fob-watch. "The press are due here in just under an hour, to witness this astonishing piece of history, this amazing revelation I have reconstructed from my vast and careful research into how the Resurrection Temple of Pharaoh Bonelaten would have originally appeared."

"The press?"

"Arrr. After a brisk tour of the site, they shall be led in here. They will read this carving of astonishment, and report the amazing proclamation to the world – to every far-flung corner, to every extremity! And then,

in a few short weeks, when my luxuriant beard has grown back handsomely, I shall emerge from the 'After Life' and take my rightful place as the most powerful individual of all time!"

Desdemona looked at him, her eyes red with admiration. "You're really gonna pull it off this time," she croaked. "What a plan!"

"Hmm," he frowned, pulling the rope that was around the Spiffystone wall. "The corner of this Most Hallowed Resurrection Prediction Wall isn't sitting very well on those few slabs down there. They're a bit uneven. Before the press arrives, you had better just dig a bit of sand from under those slabs, Desdemona, to give the wall a firmer foundation..."

For many minutes, Jim, Doris and Brenda continued making their way along the tunnel.

They walked and fluttered silently, shining their torches along the roughly plastered, undecorated walls, and illuminating every place where they thought they might find a clue as to what this tunnel might lead to. But nothing showed up in their torchbeams – no chinks or small openings or ledges. The walls continued to creep along into the earth, and judging from the steady, unwavering gloom ahead, it seemed that they were to go on forever.

Jim's Sahara boots echoed as he trudged along the hard-earth floor.

Doris's wings *flooooshed* through the cool, stale air

 197

as she made her way through the tunnel.

Brenda snorted every now and again into the darkened space before them.

And then, after what seemed like a lifetime to the archaeologist, macaw and Wonder Camel, the gloom in the distance began to change.

"Rerk!" Doris rerked quietly. "Look, up there, it's not quite as dark!"

Jim stopped walking and squinted. "That's strange," he muttered. "It's *not* quite as dark as here." He shone his torch all around the tunnel in front of him.

"The tunnel's opening out," thought Brenda. "Getting wider."

"The tunnel's opening out," announced Doris. "Getting wider."

"That it is," agreed Jim. "But the area beyond ... it's not as gloomy as here, yet there's no new light in there. Why does it look different, then?"

"One way to find out." Doris stretched her wings and flew towards the wider section of tunnel. With a strange feeling of weightlessness in Jim's legs and in Brenda's humps, they both followed her.

The beating of Doris's wings stopped when she saw it. She hovered for a moment in the air, squawkless, before descending to the floor.

When Brenda saw it, she trembled as a tornado of astonishment ripped through her body.

Cairo Jim was the last to see it. His eyes moved up it, up and up and up, until his neck was craned so far back his pith helmet toppled off his head. The archaeologist-poet's jaw dropped, and his torch slid out of his hands and onto the floor. His eyes filled with a liquid excitement, and his skin burst with prickles of goosebumps.

"So *that's* why the gloom was different," he murmured in a voice that was barely his own.

"Bleccchhh!" spat Desdemona. "Have I dug enough sand out from under this slab yet?"

Mr Impluvium put on his bowler hat and smoothed down his galabiyya. "No," he answered with a sneer. "Go down another wing length or so. I want this Wall to be dead level."

The raven pecked at some fleas who were dancing a conga-line all the way down her back. She spat the dance leaders into the air.

"And then do the sand under those four slabs bordering that one," commanded Mr Impluvium. "And don't dilly-dally – the press will be here in a few minutes."

She looked up at him, her slitted eyes throbbing redly. How easy it would be to relieve him of one of his toes at this moment in time. But she thought the better of it – after all, what good would a *limping* New Saviour of the World be to anyone?

"Swoggle me spifflicatingly," gasped Cairo Jim.

Doris shook her head slowly, gobsmacked by the magnitude of it.

Brenda stared, wide-eyed, her senses quivering with the awesomeness of it.

They had left the tunnel and were now inside an enormous cavern.

In front of them stood the most incredible monument they had ever seen in their careers as archaeologists and discoverers. It was the last thing they had expected to find so far below the ground.

At first, Jim had not been able to tell what it was. The sheer height of it so overwhelmed him, all he could think was that this enormous structure must rise all the way to the very surface of the earth. And then, quite possibly, further – up into the sky above, perhaps. In his haze of flabbergastedness, he estimated that it was probably as tall as a forty-storey building.

Doris and Brenda, likewise, were so overwhelmed by the size of this thing that at first, their minds didn't even try and work out exactly what it was. The absolute hugeness of it seemed to knock the initial curiosity out of them.

After ten minutes of staring, dumbfounded at it, and after Jim's goose bumps had subsided a bit and he had picked up his torch again, and when he, Doris and Brenda had lit up every square centimetre that they could see of this colossal structure, they began to realise exactly what it was:

A pyramid, covered in bright, white limestone, every centimetre as big as the Great Pyramid of Cheops.

But, unlike the Great Pyramid of Cheops, *the apex of this pyramid was at the bottom*!

On all the sides of this structure, there was no earth or sand. Just a great, cavernous expanse of air that continued all the way up to the surface of the earth, so far above.

"It's balanced," Doris said when she could get her voice back. "It's upside-down, and balanced on its point!"

"Upside-down for us," thought Brenda. "But maybe not for those who built it?"

Herodotitis's description from Bathsheba's diary flooded into Jim's mouth and out his lips: "'More marvellous, more astonishing, more breathtakingly, ambitiously and stunningly built than all of the Seven Wonders put together. A monument so brilliantly constructed that it defies explanation.'"

"I'd say that's it," Doris cooed.

Jim licked his lips, and wiped the tears of incredulity from his eyes. Every symphony he had ever heard played all at once in his heart. "Can you *imagine*..." The words stuck in his throat; he tried again. "Can you imagine ... the knowledge they must have had ... to be able to balance ... to be able to balance *perfectly*, to the minutest of degrees, something as big as *this*?"

"Quaoooo," snorted Brenda. "If only we still had that knowledge today," she thought.

"If only we still had that knowledge today," said Doris.

"This is what Herodotitis meant when he said to tread carefully – 'greatness such as this is easily toppled'." Jim aimed his torchbeam at the uppermost part of the pyramid. The white limestone glinted startlingly in the light. "Of course," he said. "Now I know! Like we said before, we needed to see things differently. We needed to think differently, and imagine so hard that our ribs hurt!"

Doris looked at him.

He started doing a tiny jig on the spot. "My friends," he said, "do you remember how big an area the Amehetnehet stones covered?"

"Rerk! Five hectares, we estimated."

"Exactly. And how big is the base of the Great Pyramid of Cheops?"

"Five hectares," Brenda thought.

Doris clamped her wing over her eyes. "Do you mean—?"

Jim smiled, a smile so big it might well have rivalled the pyramid before them. "The stones of Amehetnehet we found up there are actually the *base* of this pyramid. The lost Pyramid of Amehetnehet!"

Doris whistled. "You've done it this time, Jim of Cairo. This is the GREATEST discovery in the whole history of archaeology!"

"No, my dear, *I* haven't done it. *We've* done it. Doris and Brenda and Jim of Cairo. We're one together, aren't we?"

"Quaooo!" Brenda rolled her head happily, and

202

her eyelashes tingled with untold pleasure.

"Look at it," Jim said proudly. "All that white limestone. The pyramids up above, on ground level, were originally covered in this, before the outer casing stones were nearly all stripped away by plunderers."

"Rotten thieves," Doris scowled.

"And I bet," continued Jim, "that like those pyramids up there, Amehetnehet's Pyramid here is made of about two million three hundred thousand blocks, with granite in the burial chamber."

"Of course!" shrieked the macaw. "There's still the inside! What treasures of Time await us in there?"

"Come on," Jim urged, "let's go find the descending passage that'll lead us in. Or I should say, the *ascending* passage. My goodness, this is the paragon of topsy-turviness if ever I saw it!"

With Doris perched on his shoulder, he led Brenda around the Pyramid of Amehetnehet. Slowly, mouse-quietly, they moved around the incredibly inverted structure, barely daring to breathe lest they should knock the pyramid from its fine point.

"That limestone down there, at the apex," Jim thought, "must be the strongest limestone ever formed. Either that, or the ancient Amehetnehet architects were able to deduce *exactly* the right amount of degrees to set each and every stone, so that the whole thing would sit absolutely perfectly." The thought made his eyebrows bristle with awe, and he felt a little dizzy.

Then, when they were passing by the third side of the pyramid, Doris gently fluttered her wing against Jim's neck. "Look," she whispered. "Up there. Just above that huge limestone gable. It's the entrance aperture!"

Jim smiled.

Brenda snorted quietly.

"Okay, gang, we're going to have to climb up for a while. It'll be the same as when we climbed the Great Pyramid of Cheops for the first time, only now it'll all be in reverse."

"Rerark! What if we overbalance the whole pyramid?" Doris's feathers bristled worriedly.

Jim surveyed the vast expanse of limestone blocks with his torch. "There's so much weight in this already," he answered, "that I doubt if the combined weight of a Wonder Camel, a macaw and an archaeologist-poet will make very much difference at all. But to be on the safe side, my dear, you'd better fly up, and Brenda and I will spread out, so that we're not putting too much weight on the one spot."

"Good thinking," Brenda thought, rolling her head and moving away from Jim.

Carefully the three of them ascended about twenty of the huge blocks, until they stood on the gable below the aperture. Jim had been right – as they went up, the pyramid moved not a millimetre.

He crouched down and shone his torch up into the slender aperture. "Look," he breathed, as though his

voice was knobbly with goosebumps. "Steps going up and up and up. They might go to the burial chamber, or, if this is like the pyramid of Chephren at Giza, they might lead up to what would be the opposite of the lower passageway entrance. That would be coming down, from below the sands."

"Coo," Doris cooed as she shone her torch up the stairs.

"Quaaaoooo!" snorted Brenda urgently.

Jim kept shining his torch up into the pyramid. "What is it, my lovely?"

"Quaaaooooooo!" she snorted again, this time more urgently.

"I think she can hear something," Doris said. "What, Bren? What can you hear?"

"Listen," the Wonder Camel implored telepathically.

"Listen," Jim said.

They were silent for a few moments, Doris's head cocked to one side, Jim's ear-holes wide open and receptive.

"Sounds like something's *moving* in there," said Doris.

"Moving?"

A noise was building, far up inside the pyramid. What it was, they couldn't be sure, but it was coming towards them.

"Sounds like a steam train," Jim muttered. "It couldn't be a steam train, all the way down here, surely?"

"Look what we're standing on," Doris squawked. "In this life, *anything's* possible!"

The sound was getting louder, coming closer, building as it seemed to slide down towards them – whooshing and thudding and bumping. A faint shrieking, like that of a whistle, grew higher and louder.

"Whatever it is, it's having a rough trip, by the sound of it!"

"*Rark!*"

Without warning, showers of sand spilled out of the aperture, followed by small rocks and a handful of glossy black feathers. The noise was nearly deafening now.

Jim, Doris and Brenda moved swiftly back, away from the aperture.

Suddenly, like a tangled wave of debris from the past, an enormous explosion of flotsam spewed out of the aperture, and bounced down the side of the pyramid of Amehetnehet in a thunderous cloud of dust and grit.

△△△△△ **22** △△△△△

THE SURFACE OF THINGS

"ARRRRR," CAME A SHAKEN MOAN from the mess. "When I said dig, I didn't mean dig all the way to China, you cretinous craterous creature!"

"What the—?" gasped Doris, shining her torch on the mess.

"I'm certain my esteemed backside slammed against every single step on the way down. Ouch!"

The rubble started to move – great fragments of Spiffystone wall, clods of rock and streams of sand. From under it all, a large man emerged, pushing bits of the Spiffystone off his chest and wiping his fingernails on his dirty and torn galabiyya. "Blast," he sneered. "It'll be three months before these fingernails are any good again."

He fished around in the mess and found a battered, dusty bowler hat, which he plonked unceremoniously onto his grit-laced hair.

Cairo Jim thought he recognised the man, but he couldn't be sure exactly who it was.

For a few seconds the eyes of Impluvium were stunned by the lights from the three torches above. He looked like a fat rabbit caught in a car's headlights. As he raised his arm to cover his eyes, he spied Jim,

Doris and Brenda on the limestone above him. He got to his feet hurriedly. "Arrr," he frowned. "I *thought* I detected the acrid stench of unbridled optimism!"

"Who are you?" shouted Jim.

Brenda came close to Jim and nuzzled around in his knapsack.

"He looks familiar," Doris whispered.

"Impluvium!" Jim decided. "That's how Perry described him to us – that galabiyya and the hat, why, no on else would be seen dead—"

"Shut your goody-goody platitude hole," snarled Impluvium.

"That voice," said Jim. "I know that voice!"

Brenda pulled out her disguise and thrust it from her snout into Jim's hand.

"No, my lovely, this isn't the time for dress-ups, this is—" It dawned on him what the Wonder Camel was trying to tell him. "You mean he's in disguise?"

"Arrrr," arrrred Bone. The rubble next to him shifted, and a dirty black wing shoved a bit of Spiffystone architrave away. A beak appeared, then a rough yellow tongue, and then two throbbing eyes the colour of blood.

"Sqwweeerkk!" shrieked Doris. "The fleabag!"

"Bone!" Jim cried.

"In all my greatness," he purred through his flabby lips.

"You're not dead?"

"What do I look like – a toffee apple? No, Cairo-Goody-Boy, I am not dead. My 'demise' was

merely a brilliant concoction of destiny. I must say *I* am surprised to see the three of *you*, though. I thought you would have left the country by now, in your state of absolute disgrace! You underhanded charlatan, Jim!"

Doris's blood began to boil. "How dare you, you multiple-chinned monstrosity! You set Jim up! You concocted the whole thing, you evil, bloated—"

"CLAMP THAT BEAK, YOU FEATHERED EXCUSE FOR A PIN-CUSHION! Or I shall set my friend here onto you."

Desdemona's eyes throbbed with delight. "Let me at her, let me at her, oh please? I could remove those gaudy feathers in three seconds!"

"All in bad time, Desdemona." Bone's eyes beheld the vast pyramid before him. "Hmmm," he said. "Not bad. Not bad at all. When did you knock all this up, you fake?"

Jim could feel himself burning with a fury he had never felt for this man before. He was so enraged, he could not speak.

"We *discovered* it," Doris squawked. "Thanks to the Diary of Bathsheba Snugg and the writings of Herodotitis!"

"Quaaaooo," Brenda agreed.

"You mean," snarled Bone, "that *I* discovered it. Me. Mr Impluvium, while painstakingly reconstructing the impressive Resurrection Temple of Bonelaten." His eyes flashed greedily as he took in the magnificence. "This will certainly add credibility to my resurrection."

Jim could stand no more. "Right," he said quickly to Doris and Brenda. "Come on, let's race up these stairs and into the world again. We'll blow his story sky-high!"

"OH NO YOU WON'T!" In a flash, Bone had reached under his galabiyya and extracted from his garter a small silver implement. It looked like a kitchen knife as he held it betwixt his pudgy fingers.

"Rerk! What're you planning to do with *that*? Butter some toast?"

Bone's eyes glinted as he pressed a small button on the handle of the implement. With a tiny *swiiiish*, the implement extended to eighty times its original size. With both hands he held the broad, curved blade triumphantly above his head.

"One should always travel with one's Indomitarbel Telescopic Scimitar," he growled. "Don't move a muscle or feather, any of you. This can slice a brick at forty paces."

"You don't scare us, Bone," Jim shouted, his voice wavering.

"I warn you, one movement and I shall cut off the very tip of this pyramid. Clean through! And then, if my knowledge of underground physics is accurate, the whole thing will topple, causing a major earthquake on the Giza plateau. Then the entire city of Cairo will slide southwards into the Aswan Dam, resulting in the biggest, most catastrophic tidal wave on the River Nile, and a surge of destruction that will not only wipe out all of the eastern countries of Africa, but will change the climatic conditions for the rest of the entire continent, and shall have a ripple effect that will destroy the economies of three-quarters of the known world! Arrrrrrr!"

"You don't do anything by halves, do you?" said Jim.

"Enough! Desdemona, rip some cloth from the hem of my garment, enough to gag and bind the three of 'em!"

"Aye, aye, my Captain! A pleasure indeed!" She set to work with her razor-sharp beak.

"Be careful of my kneecaps, bird, they are extremely precious. Then, when you've trussed the felons, tie them together with this piece of rope from my Most Hallowed Resurrection Prediction Wall. And hurry. We have to get up all those steps with our captives as quickly as possible. We have a date with the press, far, far above us, where once and for all, Cairo Jim and his friends will finish their days in much-deserved disgrace!"

The time had come for the press of the world to arrive, and arrive they had, en masse and with a surge of enthusiasm.

Thousands of men and women (and a few dogs) from every television network, every radio empire, every newspaper and magazine enterprise in the world were thronging at the eastern perimeter of the reconstructed Resurrection Temple of Pharaoh Bonelaten. A forest of Spiffystone columns, arches, passageways, colonnades, ziggurats, aqueducts, fountains, statues and sunken vestibules glinted in the sunlight.

The men and women (and their dogs) of the press were suitably impressed – many photos being taken and film footage being shot. But there was growing impatience at the non-appearance of Mr Impluvium, the man responsible for it all.

At last he appeared, dusty and battered, leading a trussed-up bundle from out of one of the many colonnades.

"There he is!" shouted one of the reporters.

All attention turned to Mr Impluvium as he removed his hat and wiped his sweaty brow (the stairs had not been an easy climb for the obese man). With a flick of his thumb, the Telescopic Scimitar shrank to its butter-knife size, and he quickly threw it behind a Spiffystone sphinxette.

"Ladies and gentlemen" – he was puffing heavily – "and everyone else of the global press, WELCOME to the unveiling of the vast and grand Resurrection Temple of Pharaoh Bonelaten! Please forgive my dishevelled appearance, but I have, just this morning, made a new discovery of the most astonishing proportion!"

Jim looked over his shoulder at Doris and Brenda, who were tied close to his side and back. His mouth was gagged by a strip of the stinking, unwashed cloth from Impluvium's galabiyya, but his eyes were wide.

Brenda could not even utter a snort.

Doris gave her friends a worried wink and moved her mandible back and forth, working away at the cloth around her beak.

"But before I tell you of this amazing new find," Impluvium continued, "look what I also discovered!"

At that moment, two patrol cars from the Antiquities Squad pulled up at the back of the crowd. A handful of Antiquities Squad Inspectors clambered out of the cars, led by Chief Inspector Reg Apollo.

Impluvium flung his pudgy arm at the trussed-up trio. "Behold, fresh from their subterranean skulking place, that charlatan archaeologist who tried to fool us all by claiming that these stones beneath us were a genuine ancient discovery – Cairo Jim, and his colleagues, Dolly the macaw and Bender the Wonder Camel!"

A growl moved through the crowd of press people, and mutterings of 'Liars', 'Traitors', 'We'll show them' and 'The bare-faced shame' could be heard dotting the swell of unrest.

Jim struggled against the coarse rope around his arms and torso, but it was no use – he was bound too tightly.

Chief Inspector Reg Apollo led his men through the throng, flashing his Antiquities Squad badge to ensure easy access. "Cairo Jim," he said gravely. "We've been wanting to question you for a while now, in relation to this hoax of the Amehetnehet stones."

Jim tried to display his innocence by a frantic manipulation of his sweat-streaked eyebrows.

"Arrr," Impluvium blurted. "Yes, Inspector, question

him you must. And then you must lock him up, him and his friends there, in the most hopeless, desolate cell you have. There is no worse crime of passion than when a formerly honourable man turns to the world of deception for his own personal gains!"

"Here, here!" cried a large contingent of the press. "Lock them away, lock them away for ever!"

Doris gave a final thunk of her jaw, and the tip of her beak tore through the cotton gag. Quickly she manoeuvred the tip around until there was a hole big enough for her to open her beak fully.

With the fire in her belly of a thousand outrages, she squawked for all her life:

"RAAAAAAAAARRRRRRR?KKKKKKKK! Don't believe a lying word of his! That's not Mr Impluvium, that's Neptune Flannelbottom Bone!"

The press people stopped muttering and looked at her. Reg Apollo stroked his strong chin and frowned.

"Poppycock!" Impluvium scoffed blusteringly. "I am Mr Impluvium, of the Baltimore Impluviums, a family with a long—"

"He shaved off his beard, and put on those clothes!" Doris screeched. "Look at the colour combination – dreadful!"

"That is a serious allegation," said Reg Apollo.

"Rerk, I can prove it's Bone!"

"We all know that Bone is dead. He perished on the island of Samos. His remains have already been interred at the Old Relics Society."

"A hoax, a hoax!" Doris started flexing up and down beneath the rope. "He staged his own death!"

"Ha! *They* should talk about hoaxes." Impluvium pointed his pudgy chins at the trussed-up trio. "Look at what we're standing on, the biggest potential hoax—"

Apollo raised his hand. "Desist, please, sir. Let Doris speak. After all, she was once trustworthy, as were her colleagues."

"Still am!" shrieked the macaw. "Still are, all three of us. I'll prove he's Neptune Bone. Listen to me." She took a deep breath and caught Jim's worried eye. "Don't worry, buddy-boy," she whispered to him. "I've thought this through."

"Go on, we're waiting," Apollo said.

"Okey-dokey. The mother of Captain Neptune Flannelbottom Bone was a tea bag recycler!"

Mr Impluvium listened silently, but those closest to him detected a slight tinge of scarlet creeping across his fat neck.

"Furthermore," Doris continued, "the mother of Neptune Flannelbottom Bone drank cheap sherry through a straw at eight o'clock in the morning! And in the nude!"

A general sound of distaste rose from the press. Still Mr Impluvium said nothing, but the scarlet started to rise into the lower of his sixteen chins.

"And," Doris added loudly, "the mother of Neptune Flannelbottom Bone, despite being wealthy, used to raid charity bins for her clothes!"

Now all of Impluvium's chins were scarlet.

"Plus, the mother of Neptune Flannelbottom Bone used to ride trams and buses and trains without once paying her fare!"

The chubby cheeks of Impluvium were changing hue.

"And the mother of Neptune Flannelbottom Bone used to cut her toenails in public places!"

His nostrils were flaring wider and wider, and his breathing was getting louder.

"But who could ever forget that the mother of Neptune Flannelbottom Bone was a dedicated torturer of molluscs?"

A certain forehead was brilliant vermilion with rage.

"And that she dressed her son just like Shirley Temple until he was fifteen years old?"

"RIGHT!" Impluvium turned on his heel, a look of gross hatred making his eyes bulge. "YOU DISGUST-ING FEATHERED FREAK, HOW DARE YOU SLANDER MY—"

"See? See? It *is* Bone! Only Neptune Bone would defend Bone's mother with such vehemence!"

"Quickly," Apollo commanded his men, "untie Jim, Doris and Brenda!"

With the aid of their Archaeological Felon Deterrent Pocket-knives, the Squad slashed through the ropes and gags.

Jim, Doris and Brenda shook off the ropes and gags and flexed their cramped limbs and wings.

A dark smudge of feathers swooped in through the columns. "Crarrrk!" rasped Desdemona. "They're not the only ones who're undone! They've got us this time, my Captain!"

Bone looked at all the press people before him, and saw the rage in their faces – this second hoodwinking was obviously bothering them more than the first.

The Antiquities Squad was inching forward, Apollo taking a pair of silver handcuffs and bronze wingcuffs from his blazer. "I've waited a long time for you," he seethed at the sweating bulk of human panic.

Bone had to think fast. Suddenly he saw his salvation. "Look! Up there in the sky! Oh my goodness gracious me! That cloud! It's in the exact shape of Mustafa Kemal Ataturk, the famous Turkish person!"

The eyes of the press all turned skyward – this was too good an opportunity to pass up, and their editors and news programmers would reward them handsomely for such a story, as had happened so often in the past.

Even the members of the Antiquities Squad looked at the spectacle.

"So it is," gasped Cairo Jim. "Well, swoggle me in cotton wool and call me cumulus!"

"Quaoooo," Brenda snorted urgently. "They're getting away!"

Bone had ripped off his galabiyya, snatched up the telescopic scimitar, extended it to its full length, and he and the raven were hurtling through the crowd, towards Jocelyn Osgood's tethered montgolfier balloon, near the remains of Cairo Jim's campsite.

"Arrrr, fly on ahead, Desdemona, and get the burner ignited!"

"Aye aye!" She whoooshed off ahead of him.

"Quickly!" shouted Reg Apollo. "Apprehend them!"

Bone pushed a large television cameraman who was busy filming the strange cloud formation. The cameraman fell onto the cameraman next to him, and he onto the one next to him. On through the crowd, cameramen and camerawomen fell, like a collapsing line of dominoes, their arms and cameras flying out and knocking down entire lines and clusters of media people.

Apollo and his men had to jump over the fallen masses. "Hurry! As fast as you can! Step over the press if you have to! This time he must *not* escape!"

Jim grabbed Brenda's saddle and, gently but swiftly, hoisted himself up and onto her back. Doris jumped up onto the pommel. "Okay, my lovely," he urged. "Let's go scum-hunting!"

With a fierce snort of eagerness, she galloped back, through the columns, avoiding the squirming thousands. The trio emerged at the other side of the Amehetnehet stones – the base of the greatest pyramid known to humankind – and galloped off to the balloon.

"Here I come!" Bone cried, the sweat drenching his plus-fours trousers and emerald-green waistcoat. He threw the scimitar ahead, so that it slashed through the two ropes holding the montgolfier to the ground. Then, with a burst of agility surprising for someone of his bulk, he dived forward and into the basket just as it was lifting from the ground.

"Open up the flame!" he shrieked.

"Burn, burn, burn!" Desdemona croaked. The flame leapt higher, and the montgolfier soared upwards towards the strangely shaped cloud, just as Jim, Doris and Brenda reached the spot where the balloon had been tethered.

"You overblown blimp of outrage!" yelled Jim, shaking his fist at the skybound vessel.

"Bye bye, Jim of Cairo. See you never ever ever again! Arrrr!"

"So long, suckers!" taunted the raven.

"By the way," Bone shouted as he grew smaller against the clouds, "Mother never used tea bags, new *or* recycled! She was strictly a leaf woman! Arrrrrrrr!"

"Mark my words, Bone," cried Jim, "your doings will catch up with you!"

"Mark THIS, Jim!" And he displayed a bit of himself that nobody ever wanted to see over the side of the basket, and wobbled it about haughtily.

Doris was nearly sick.

Some pistol shots rang out from the Antiquities Squad, but most of the bullets fell well short of the disappearing basket.

Everyone on the ground watched as the balloon found a pocket of fast wind and sailed off, speedily and defiantly, towards the east.

WHY WE DON'T KNOW ABOUT IT

"WELL," SAID CAIRO JIM, putting on his special desert sun-spectacles and patting Brenda's neck, "I suppose it's time to clear up all this business."

"No time like the present," chirped Doris, flexing her wings and putting the image of Neptune Bone's display out of her mind.

"Speaking of time," Jim muttered, looking at his Cutterscrog Old Timers Archaeological Timepiece, "my watch glass has smashed. Must've happened when we were coming down the Workers' Shaft." He held the wristwatch to his ear. "Stopped completely."

"Never mind," Doris prerked. "Give me your pith helmet and I'll tell you the correct time."

Jim looked confounded, but gave her his hat.

Brenda snorted smartly – she had finally worked out how the macaw did it.

Doris held the pith helmet up to the sky, peered through one of the ventilation holes, and announced, in a clever tone, "It's eleven-seventeen and thirty-six seconds exactly."

"Okay," said Jim, taking the hat from her. "You win, my dear. I'm utterly flabbergasted as to how you do it."

"So you should be," she said.

"Please tell me. Otherwise I won't sleep tonight."

The macaw hopped up onto his shoulder. "Easy, easy, easy," she chirped. "All you have to do is hold the hat up against the right part of the sky. If you position it over in *that* direction, and look through one of the holes, you can directly see the clock on the Cairo Post Office tower. It's always accurate."

She gave a loud squawk of delight, and there was a sudden *THWWWWAAAANNNNNGGGGG*! As so often happens when Doris is feeling happy with herself, her beak slapped up and locked against her eyes.

"Jmm? Ts hppnd gn. Pls cn y fx m bk?"

He reached up and, with a warm laugh, pulled her beak down and set it into place.

"Just like you've been saying, Jim," Brenda thought with a contented snort. "It's all a matter of seeing things *differently*."

Much, much later, after all the business of the Bone-Impluvium deception had been sorted out with the Antiquities Squad, and when the hideous Spiffystone sculptures had been cleared away and destroyed, Cairo Jim persuaded the Old Relics Society and the Ministry of Archaeology to cover the stones of the base of Amehetnehet's tomb with many tonnes of sand.

Why did he do this? Why did he not continue the excavation, and open it up for everyone to see?

Because he knew that there is one thing that must never be upset: the balance between the ancient world

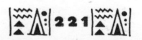

and the modern. Of all his discoveries, Cairo Jim knew that the Pyramid of Amehetnehet would be the discovery most likely to have its balance destroyed.

That is why we cannot visit this site today.

But, if ever you find yourself wandering across the sands about a thousand camel's paces south of the Pyramid of Chephren, and you accidentally drop your water bottle, and the sound it makes as it hits the sand is a hollow sort of HOOOMMMPPPPHHHHH, remember this: a man and a macaw and a Wonder Camel kept a secret, bigger than any other secret they had ever stumbled upon.

And the balance between ancient and modern – the balance of History itself – has been kept, safe and intact, buried beneath a hundred billion grains of sand.

THE END

Swoggle me sideways!
Unearth more thrilling mysteries
of history starring Cairo Jim, Doris,
and Brenda the Wonder Camel –

THE CAIRO JIM CHRONICLES

The Cairo Jim Chronicles,
read by Geoffrey McSkimming,
are available on CD
from Bolinda Audio Books!
See **www.bolinda.com** for details.